IN THE WORLD OF CONFUSION

Robert Wexelblatt

ACKNOWLEDGMENTS

"In the World of Confusion" first appeared in *The Write Room*

"The Story of My Social Life" first appeared in *Wilderness House Literary Review*

"Thyssen-Porlock Disease" first appeared in *Verdad*

"Ostbrück" first appeared in *Offcourse Literary Journal*

"Rope-Maker" and "Horatia" first appeared in *Belle Ombre*

"The Poets' Strike" first appeared in *Grasslands Review*

"The Last Philosopher" first appeared in *Lascaux Review*

"Leda Leibling" first appeared in *Five Quarterly*

"Suite Populaire Américaine" first appeared in *Blue Lake Review*

Cover Illustration: *Chaos* by Ivan Aivazovsky (1841)

Contents

IN THE WORLD OF CONFUSION

1.

"So why did you put the tomato paste in this cabinet and the tomato sauce in that one? I've told you about that a hundred times. . . . Just look in this dishwasher. You shoved my good glasses up against each other again. This one's cracked. Oh, Jesus, the knives. The knives go point up or they block the tray and scratch the door. For God's sake."

At fourteen I couldn't comprehend how I loved my parents, either how much or in what ways. I didn't appreciate that love is heterogeneous, that the word covers everything from an amicable relationship with God to a roll on a motel bed or a taste for french fries, let alone that love can be smothered underneath other feelings or wrung-out until it's faded and unrecognizable. At fourteen you feel more than you know so, though I loved my parents, this love was asphyxiated by anxiety and twisted by exasperation. As for them, I think their love for each other was being sandpapered to dust.

When the arguments began, they tried to keep them from me. Shh, she'll hear. At some point they stopped bothering.

It was the standardization of their disputes that infuriated me most. They were like religious rituals repeated by unbelievers. Mother was always the aggressor; Dad would put up about ten minutes of token resistance, then she'd come back at him twice as hard until put his head down on the table or curled up on the couch and just fell asleep.

"You're always leaving your shoes in the hall. . . . Why didn't you tell that jerk off? . . . What do you mean your forgot to pick up the cleaning?"

It wasn't tomato paste location or dishwasher protocols, it wasn't misplaced shoes or forgotten dry cleaning, of course, but that their love had turned sour and that Mother wanted out. I couldn't understand why she seemed not have caught on. Dad just didn't care, I figured, and only wanted peace which was why he went narcoleptic and made her rant even more.

I wanted to screech like her and withdraw like him. Like her, I had my grievances; like him, I wanted everything to stay the same. They were supposed to be my launching pad and you like launching pads to be stable. But then, as Baruch told me a few years later, precarious is precisely what stability always is.

Fourteen's not an easy age, at least it wasn't for me. It won't be easy for you either, I'm afraid. New breasts, the interesting boys you're interested in and the uninteresting ones that are interested in you, the worrying spirals of school, female back-biting, childhood winding up and womanhood still in the offing, years to wait for the liberation of college.

And fifteen was worse.

Worst of all were their fights about me. Mother was all for tight reins, Dad just the opposite; he had plenty of trust, but he wasn't long on principle, a feckless ally who wouldn't up a fight. What was bad wasn't that Mother was the disciplinarian but my realizing that she hated having to be.

I want it to be different for you, Miriam-I mean being an adolescent and a daughter-and I'm afraid it'll be just the same, just with smartphones and computers.

2.

I'm on maternity leave, Miriam. Miriam, we're on maternity leave. Time off for working mothers was a progressive innovation of the late twentieth century, at least in Western Europe and among a few enlightened employers or unionized workers in America. Miriam.

Miriam. If I delight in just writing your name, imagine how I love your little hands and tiny toes, the suddenness with which you've changed my life. It's just you and me all day for three months. Don't get the wrong idea, though. Daddy doesn't get any leave but he's just as nuts about you as I am, and even more scared.

So why am I writing to you who can only cry, shit, suck, burp, and smile-all of which you do gloriously? And why am I writing about my adolescence? Well, because I think some day you might be interested. I once read that no generation really gets beyond another, that emotionally we all have to start in the same place, and so when it comes to feeling we can all understand each other. It's a lovely idea and it sounds true to me; but the rub is the generations can't understand each other at the same time. When do you understand your parents? When you get to be their age, or you get to be a parent yourself? Maybe not even then. When do you understand yourself? At sixteen? When you're twenty-seven?

I've given you a Jewish name, Miriam. It's probably what Jesus' mother was called, and I chose it because it's Jewish. I expect some day this might puzzle you, since your parents aren't Jewish, or your grandparents, or your great-grandparents. Okay, so among other reasons, I'm writing this to explain your name, Miriam.

It's a long time since I've written anything, certainly something as long as this is likely to be. Not since college. Thinking of you as my reader helps. It feels funny to imagine you reading this decades from now, to wonder what you'll make of it-and of me.

3.

Both my parents worked, just like yours. For years your grandmother was the office manager for an architectural firm, the pin in their pinwheel. Dad was a product manager for a medical instrument company. So, you see, they were both managers, the irony being that, in my opinion, neither could manage. They had odd hobbies, things they didn't do together. My mother loved alpine plants. When she got email, she chose diapensia as her address. She'd drag me out of bed at dawn and make me drive up to the mountains with her. Sometimes I was glad, of course, but I didn't care for the crunchy, self-righteous hikers with whom we hooked up. My father's hobby was even higher than the mountains. He learned to fly and bought a third interest in a Cessna. I think he enjoyed being out at the airport more than flying, though. He had cronies there. They always teased me, and not very cleverly. I thought of them as the Air Bums. My point is that there wasn't much glue so far as I could see, and little balm. One night, when I couldn't block out the arguing even with my door shut and music blasting, I went to the top of the stairs and yelled down at them. "Look, if I'm the reason you two are staying together, I don't want the responsibility." I was angry and wanted to shock them. "Half the kids in my class have divorced parents so it's no big deal to me," I added. But it was. I just didn't know what to do with all those negative ions zipping around the house like gamma rays. I wasn't much of a rebel. I had a horror of drugs and just as much of sex. So, I huddled in my room and read nineteenth-century novels, the longer the better; my vocabulary swelled and my grades went up. Some rebel.

Sweet Sixteen is an American thing. Once it was about being a virgin (as you will be!), then it turned into a party for getting your learner's permit. Hispanic girls have their shindigs at fifteen, Jewish girls at thirteen. Really, it's just an occasion for the biggest party you get until your wedding, something to look forward to and worry over. It's also a chance some parents take to show off and make it look like love. I could happily have done without a party. My parents weren't the showing-off type and I had an aversion to being conspicuous. Nevertheless, I'd been invited to four of these things that year, two of them pretty extravagant, so it was expected we'd do something. Naturally, this became another casus belli for my parents. I wanted to suggest we invite the neighbors in and merge celebrations: I could hold up my learner's permit and they could hoist their separation agreement-a dj would do; no need for a band.

As it turned out, I had a small party at home, with a striped tent in the yard and a few of those long sub sandwiches and pizzas. I got to choose ten friends and my parents picked the relatives. There were some nice presents. In fact, this whole tract, Miriam, is really about one of those sweet sixteen gifts.

It was from my Uncle Albert. There may be a snapshot of him in an album somewhere, so maybe you'll get a look at him if the album survives, and you can track it down. I'd only seen Albert three times in my life, but he was my favorite relative by far. The first time I was too young to remember. The second I got a huge crush on him. He was tall and slim with shiny, slicked-back hair. He wore elegant clothing and was kind to me, the way men who spoil barren wives can be. To me, he was like the old movie stars; he was Fred Astaire, Cary Grant, David Niven, a natural aristocrat. He lived in glamorous Los Angeles with my mother's older sister, Grace, her third husband and the only one to stick it out more than a year. Grace was nothing like my mother. She was a self-centered hedonist who made awful paintings and was immune to discipline. To everybody's astonishment, Albert stayed married to Grace for the rest of his life, apparently quite happily.

The third time I saw Albert I was twelve and full of embarrassing anticipation the moment I learned he was in town. He and Aunt Grace were making a royal progress down the East Coast to Palm Beach. They didn't crowd in with us, of course. They stayed in a five-star hotel. Aunt Grace called as soon as they got in and insisted we all meet at her favorite downtown restaurant to eat lobsters. "My sister always has to have lobster when she comes home," Mother said bitterly. I shared my mother's view of Aunt Grace; I thought her a frivolous woman unworthy of Albert and couldn't understand why he doted on her, treating her, I couldn't help noticing, much the way he did me. How infantile she looked in her paper bib at the big round table. Uncle Albert and I sat next to one another. I ordered baked scallops and, gallantly, he did the same. Forgoing lobster made a bond.

Over our scallops Albert regaled me with the glories of Southern California and how, when I came to visit, we'd go to the beach, then up to the mountains, then over the border to Mexico. We'd visit his friends at the movie studios, too. Golden promises. I never did get an invitation, though. Maybe my aunt didn't care for houseguests or me.

Grace and Albert got a courtesy invitation to my Sweet Sixteen. My aunt couldn't or wouldn't come, but Albert phoned to say he had to fly east on business and would arrange the timing. He said he'd adore to see his little niece Olivia all grown up.

He arrived in a taxi wearing a beautiful gray suit and a purple silk tie. He was carrying a wicker basket with a puppy in it, a little black thing with a disproportionately large head and wonderful dark eyes. I'd never had a real pet. Mother wouldn't countenance the mess and responsibility of a dog, and cats made my father sneeze. But I was sixteen now and I think they were sort of intimidated by my uncle. The puppy was a Scottish terrier and, like any kind of puppy, irresistible. I took the basket in my arms, set it down on the grass outside the tent, and the little thing hopped right out and licked my face for all it was worth. He didn't try to lick anybody else; he never did, in fact. When I set him down, he walked backwards. Albert explained that Scotties were bred to go into holes after rats and foxes and pull them out, so they're naturally inclined to walk backwards before they walk forwards. Maybe he made that up on the spot. Anyway, I assumed he was an authority on his present and he assured me that my puppy would soon be walking forwards, and so he did.

I asked if the dog already had a name. Albert said no. Picking a name, he said grandly, was my privilege. That was the word he used, privilege. I'd never named anything before. My girlfriends gathered around and set up the sort of mawkish row girls make over anything newborn and then they began suggesting names, competing to be the cutest: Boopsy, Teeny, Burns, Kiltie, Glasgow, Jock, Morrison, Dundee, Bobby as in Dylan, Jimmy as in Dean. But I felt naming this tiny being was a serious responsibility, and I wasn't about to rush it, let alone relinquish it.

Albert had to leave early. He was flying somewhere at dawn. I never saw him again; he died of a heart attack two months later and, six months after that, Aunt Grace, for reasons I thought I understood without approving, knocked back a glass of vodka and a couple handfuls of sleeping pills.

After the party finally guttered out, I thanked the guests for coming, my parents for the party, then said I'd be taking the puppy up to my room. Mother objected. She wanted him locked in the downstairs bathroom, which she called the Powder Room, with newspapers spread three deep all over the floor. I took an armful of newspapers and did as I was told. Mom and Dad cleaned up, so worn out from hosting that they didn't even argue with each other. Once they'd gone to bed, I tiptoed downstairs. There were whimpers coming from under the bathroom door. I opened it as quietly as I could. The puppy trembled with delight at seeing me and I smuggled him up to my bedroom.

I sat cross-legged on the bed, my chin propped thoughtfully on my palm. He looked up at me, full of expectation, cocking his head fetchingly.

"What am I going to call you?" I said.

He uncocked his head. "How about Zev or Dov? No, better yet, Baruch. Baruch. How's that?"

Then he waggled his bottom and panted up at me, all doggy ingratiation. "Okay?"

I was tired, way too tired. I figured I must have been hallucinating. I turned out the light, patted his head, and in no time we both fell asleep.

4.

At dawn, there was more face-licking. He'd also made a mess on the floor, some of which had, by accident, gotten on the newspaper I laid down the night before.

I frowned at the little charmer.

"I'm sorry," he said. "Couldn't help it."

I shivered. "Are you really talking or am I wacko?"

"I can talk but I can't control myself. I'm too young-well, and also too old."

"Mom!" I screamed.

He put a little paw on my arm. "Shh. You want them to think you're crazy?"

"I think I'm crazy!"

"Well, you're not."

"But-"

"But nothing. I talk only to you. Nobody else. Got it?"

"What?"

"Can I have maybe a little something to eat?"

"I want to tell. I have to. I'm your owner, your mistress. You're supposed to obey me."

"For the most part, sure. Look, I really want something to eat or I'm going to start yowling. I won't be able to help that either."

"Stop chewing that blanket."

"I'm a puppy. It comes naturally."

"I've lost my mind."

"Please believe me, you haven't. Food!"

My thoughtful uncle had brought a bag of puppy kibble. I went downstairs and put some in a bowl and covered it with warm tap water. My hands trembled.

Baruch had done some serious damage to the blanket by the time I got back. "I don't know how to jump yet. Put me down next to that bowl, please. I could eat a poodle."

I lifted him from the bed with one hand. He dived into the bowl, little tail motoring like mad.

The party was on a Saturday night. I spent the next day alone with my puppy, with Baruch. Dad left early for the airport and coffee with the Air Bums while Mom had a brunch and a garden tour with her comrades from the Horticultural Society. I found out a lot that day, not everything, not yet, but it began with the discovery that a rolled-up pair of old knee-socks was Baruch's ideal toy. He treated it like a caught rat, a little fox, chasing it, pulling it backwards, shaking his adorable Scottie head back and forth, as if to break the thing's neck. I was relieved that, while there was a good deal of high-pitched growling, there was no rational discourse and figured that whatever somebody had put in the pizza the night before must have worn off. My relief was premature.

I took him out in the backyard. I sat under the maple tree and tossed the socks for him and experimented with endearments. It was all going normally enough until he dropped the knee-socks and rolled over, inviting me to rub his belly.

"That good?" I crooned complacently.

"Terrific. Look, Olivia, I'm not a man trapped in a dog's body, you know. That's what you were thinking last night, isn't it? But you wanted to pretend it never happened. Come on, am I right or am I right?"

I pulled my hand back as if I'd been stung.

"What? You're thinking Frog Prince?"

"It's better than thinking I'm loony. Anyway, aren't you? I mean something like the Frog Prince? God, I can't believe I'm saying this."

He rolled onto on his stumpy Scottie legs and walked backward. "Not everything all at once, okay? I'm just a puppy and you've just turned sixteen. Let's take it slow."

"What's that supposed to mean?"

He sniffed around the trunk of the maple and tried out a few forward steps.

"I don't understand," I said.

"You think I do?"

"What?"

"Be patient. I understand a little."

"Are you a dog or not?"

"Oh, I'm a dog all right. I'm completely a dog. I've got doggy thoughts and urges and needs. I'm utterly desperate for you to love me and that proves I'm a dog. Getting the right person to love you is life and death for a dog, you know. The thing is-"

"What's the thing?"

"Well, apparently I'm not only a dog."

"Obviously! So what? You're a frog and a prince?"

"It's no fairy tale, at least not to me."

"Reincarnated then, is that it?"

"Do I look like a Hindu?"

His sarcasm exasperated me. "How should I know? Are you a Scotsman?"

"That's a laugh." He barked convincingly.

"What then?"

"I wasn't reborn as a dog, no."

"Who's I?"

He rolled on the ground, tried going forward again, gave my hand a little lick, cavorted-all, I figured, his way of changing the subject.

"Who are you?"

"I'm your puppy, Baruch."

"And?"

"Try to imagine that the thing that loves you so much somehow got smushed into a dog's brain. The dog and the thing that loves you, has always loved you, they're right up tight in here, inseparable even."

"How?"

He sat on his haunches and looked as pensive as a puppy can. "Why do people assume the dead know all about death? Do the living know all about life?"

"You're dead?"

"Yes and no," he said and piddled on the maple tree. "It's hard to be certain, but I'm pretty sure I'm dead. I'd have to be, wouldn't I? At my age."

"You're old?"

"Very. The kind of old where you lose count."

I sighed. "Can you at least tell me why you'll only talk to me? Do you know what that's going to do to me, what it's already doing?"

"It's a secret. Don't young girls have lots of secrets?"

"Sure, but-"

"Just as I thought." He pushed his head against my leg. I'd already learned this meant I was to scratch behind his ears.

"I wasn't finished," I said, scratching. "We have secrets yes, but not from everybody. And certainly not one like this."

He gave a little puppy shrug. "Secrets are secrets."

I stopped scratching. "You're not listening. This secret separates me from everyone. Girls have secrets so they can share them with other girls. That's half their point, to share them."

"So, secrets connect girls? That's odd."

"We whisper a lot. We pass notes. We share."

"Well, that's all right then," he said brightly. "You are sharing. With me."

I threw up my arms. "I mean with somebody human."

He turned his little rear-end on me. "I'm going to practice walking forward now."

There was no more talking that day, just unalloyed puppiness.

With my parents, I observed, Baruch, either out of calculation or instinct, was determined to establish working relationships-cordial, yet reserved. He liked it when my father mumbled "good boy" at him and when my mother called him "cute"; but, starting with that leap of faith out of the basket, he left no doubt that he was a one-girl dog. A matter of life and death, he'd said.

Further information was not forthcoming the next day either. When I rushed in from school, he was rapturous; I was his liberator. Mother had incarcerated him all day in the downstairs bathroom where he'd overturned his bowl of water, perhaps in protest. The knee-socks, which

I called "Foxy-Lox," appeared to have received considerable attention. While I cleaned up after him, he kept as close to me as he could, leech-like with pure love and the terror of being abandoned. It had not been a happy day for Baruch; but he'd made good progress in walking forward. I congratulated him and got no reply but a wagging tail and a hanging tongue. I felt silly, waiting for him to say something, but also saner and I phoned two of my friends for some normal gossip. Watching me talk into a little piece of plastic seemed to enthrall and perplex him; there was a quantity of head-cocking.

That night my parents arrived home within half an hour of each other, as usual. Dad was always second, as if he'd been hiding outside that extra thirty minutes mustering the nerve to come in. Thanks in part to the distraction of my puppy, things went pretty smoothly until almost the end of dinner. After Baruch had greeted her with recognition and even some gallantry, after she couldn't find anything in tatters or a yellow stain on a carpet or a turd in a closet, Mom lightened up. Dad greeted Baruch like an old poker pal, handed me a small bag of dog treats, sat me down, and pompously offered me advice on housebreaking: "If he goes on the kitchen floor he gets a newspaper across the nose; if he uses the yard-or, better yet-the park, he gets a treat. Easy. Pavlov." I turned to Baruch and made a couplet: "Hear that? Kitchen means switchin'; street means treat."

The arguing broke out suddenly and had nothing to do with me or the puppy. In fact, my mother's grievance was so ancient and obscure I couldn't make out what it was about. I couldn't understand the words, but I understood the music. I scooped Baruch up and headed upstairs, away from the Beethovenian thunderstorm.

I dropped Baruch on my bed, put my hands on my hips, and stared at him.

"Look," I said, feeling a little angry myself, "it's got to be clearer. Do you talk or don't you?"

He settled on the bed, full-length, making himself comfortable, letting me know that my bed was the best place on the planet. "That happen often, does it?"

"What?"

"Downstairs. The fighting."

"More and more."

He gave me a rather human nod, as if I'd just confirmed what he'd suspected all along. "So, tell me, were you disappointed about my not talking?"

I considered this. I wasn't sure. "Does it matter?"

"It matters to me."

I sat on the edge of the bed, patted his head, and changed the subject. "What did you mean about being dead?"

"I'll tell you a story. Maybe a story will help. With some things stories are the best you can do."

"Is it going to be long? I've got Algebra and English to do. Quadratic equations and Katherine Mansfield."

"Okay, I'll make it snappy. But I'm warning you, it's a Jewish story. Do you mind?"

"Why should I mind?"

"Well, your parents named you Olivia and they didn't exactly leap up and do a hora over your calling me Baruch, did they? You think I didn't hear? 'But that's a Jewish name,' your mother said. Just like that. Jewish, as if she'd smelled a bad egg. 'Have you been reading Spinoza?' your father said. They weren't exactly pleased."

"I don't care. Just tell the story, please."

"Okay, you got it. Once upon a time there was a widow who lived in a little Jewish village in Eastern Europe. She had only one son and by scrimping she got enough together to send him to study with the tzaddik Dov Baer in Mezritch. He was called the Great Maggid. This was more than two centuries ago, just so you know."

"What's a tzaddik? What's a maggid?"

"You want this to go fast, or you want footnotes?"

I rolled my eyes. "Go on."

"Well, a year after the boy went to Mezritch he fell ill. Dov Baer got a message-you know, from up above-that the boy would live only if his mother could be with him by the Sabbath. Reb Baer couldn't go himself. He had to send someone for her at once, but the only person on hand was a carter named Yitzak Wolfsheim, a terrible sinner. But Reb Baer sent for him anyway and ordered him to fetch the mother back before sundown on Friday. It was already Wednesday. Yitzak, who was afraid of the rabbi, hitched up his two nags and set out for the shtetl where the widow lived, cursing all the way. He arrived late Thursday night and had to wake people all over the village to ask the way to the widow's broken-down hovel. When he delivered his message, she screamed and insisted that they leave at once. Yitzak said that his horses were exhausted. They couldn't possibly leave before first light. The widow begged, but Yitzak wouldn't budge. He went outside and hobbled the horses then curled up on the floor and fell sleep. At dawn, the widow shook him awake and off they went. The boy's mother was beside herself. 'Faster! Faster!' she urged Yitzak who ground his teeth but whipped his horses. Did he feel for the widow and the sick boy? Perhaps. Anyway, he drove his horses so hard that one of the poor beast's hearts gave out from the strain. The widow began to wail. 'Don't you worry,' said the carter, 'I've still got the one horse.' He said this to calm her, though he didn't believe they could possibly make it Mezritch before sundown. He unhitched his dead horse and left it right there on the road and off they went again. 'Faster!' cried the widow in her desperation. And somehow Yitzak drove his one remaining horse so hard that they made it to Mezritch two hours before sundown. It was almost a miracle. The woman ran straight to her son who, at the touch of his mother's hand on his forehead, revived. Dov Baer said a prayer and made ready a thanksgiving feast for the Sabbath. They were all at the table, just breaking up the challah-"

"Challah?"

"Shh, it's special bread. So, the candles are lit and everybody's about to eat-the rabbi's whole court, his students, the widow and her son-when a late arrival comes in and says Yitzak's remaining horse's heart had given out too. The tzaddik knew that Yitzak's livelihood depended on his horses and he instructed one of his followers to go to the carter and tell him that he had done well and they would take up a collection and buy him two new horses. But the messenger came back and said that the carter's heart had also given out from the strain of his journey and anguish at the loss of his two horses. And so, sadness fell on the company. And the rabbi said kaddish, which is a solemn prayer for the dead."

"It's a sad story, but what has it got to do with you?"

"There's more. Can the equations wait?"

"Should I say 'faster' too?"

"Very funny. So, Yitzak the carter and sinner finds himself facing the heavenly court. He's done so many bad things and so few good ones that there's a whole gang of accusing angels jostling each other. All his bad acts are laid out and they're so numerous and so bad that the court's about to send him straight to eternal darkness. But then a single defending angel rises and tells the story I've just told you. The Court's perplexed. They can't send him to paradise, not with all the bad things he's done, but neither do they want to send him into nothingness, on account of the widow and her son. So they compromise. They send him to the Olam ha-Dimyon."

"What?"

"The World of Confusion. They decide that he won't know he's dead and they'll give him a new cart with two fine stallions and set him out on a wide road and in good weather too."

"He's going to be driving forever? And all alone?"

"I suppose he might have. He was happy to get off so lightly. He was content. But Dov Baer learned of the heavenly judgment and lodged an appeal. He wasn't called the Great Maggid for nothing. He sends people to find the carter and bring him to his court. The man is found and Dov Baer tells him he is dead. Yitzak didn't believe him, of course, but then the tzaddik showed him the shroud under his overcoat and said a special prayer and the carter instantly vanished into paradise. For the tzaddik's sake, you understand, but mostly for the sake of the one good deed."

"So you. . . ?"

"Am in the Olam ha-Dimyon. At least I think I am. I must be, though it doesn't make any sense. The way I understand it, the instant you know you're in the Olam ha-Dimyon then you're no longer in it, like the carter. But here I am anyway."

"But why as a dog? Why my dog?"

"Why a dog I also don't know. As for you-that's because I'm your great-great-great-grandfather, Olivia."

5.

Jennifer Alvarez started a nasty rumor about me. Mr. Dalhousie gave my paper on Dubliners a B+. My favorite TV show was canceled.

A rock singer I liked overdosed. Elena's mother was diagnosed with breast cancer. I got a part-time job in a pharmacy and didn't like my boss, Mr. Hogg. Meanwhile, my parents kept grinding away at the same raw spots on a daily basis.

Sixteen, as I expect you'll discover, my dear, is a heroic, whining age, one of negative self-definition, haunted by an insecurity you expose on pain of social death. It's caring about things you know are trivial and despising yourself for it. It's feeling worse about one pimple than four days of cramps, or war and starving children in the torrid zone. It's imagining some future exaltation, not middle-aged contentment, not bland settling, but some nebulous yet intense fulfillment, happy or sad hardly matters.

Baruch was beside me through it all, listening, licking, impeccably housebroken, always ready for a walk, perpetually ecstatic to see me.

One night, after I'd burst into tears for no good reason, I asked him, "Why do you love me so much?"

"Love's never reasonable," he said sententiously, "though people always want reasons for it. Now I love you because I know you, but the truth is I loved you long before you were born-before your father and mother were born."

"Then it couldn't have been me you loved because I didn't exist. You loved me as an idea, on principle, as a possibility, a descendant. It's like saying you'd love anybody with even one of your genes."

"That's so awful?"

"To me it's selfish. It's impersonal. What if you didn't like me when we met?"

"But I did! I was a puppy and you smelled just right."

"I still think it's kind of vain, the way people love their children and grandchildren."

"Your parents love you. They can't get over you, in fact. Anyway, it's built-in; it's just how things work. Babies and puppies need help. Love guarantees protection."

"Protection?"

"It's tough out there in the world. If that Doberman around the corner attacked you, what do you suppose I'd do? What are these teeth for if not to protect you?"

"You'd kill to protect me?"

"Without hesitation. Why? You want to give me a try?"

"No. It's just such a responsibility."

"For you and me both, Olivia. Now, what about a treat?"

6.

The pattern was set. Baruch would be silent for as long as a week, during which time he was simply all dog. I could talk to him as much as I liked, pose questions, and he'd just cock his head. Meanwhile, my parents became accustomed to having him around. My father even asked to take him out for walks. When we were in the car, my mother put the window down for him; and, when he got sick, she came with me to the vet. I had to drag him inside, yanking on his leash. Baruch explained later that the place stank of death. To him, the clinic was nothing but a dolled-up abattoir, a place people took the pets they wanted to be rid of. For a week after, he whined and flattened himself when we walked near the Honda.

During one of his talkative phases, Baruch explained about the Jewishness and where it went. He himself was a Jew, of course. An Ostjude, he said. Married twice, the second time not so happily. His first wife he extolled. Her name was-can you guess?-Miriam. Yes, that's who you're named after, your great-great-great-grandmother who died at thirty-one, deep in darkest nineteenth century. He said he wasn't entirely sure what country his village had been in because it changed owners so often: Poland, Moldava, Russia, Austro-Hungary. He couldn't figure out why Jews thought it was a good idea to set up housekeeping between Germany and Russia. "Could be," he said, "we had no more choice than the Poles."

He filled in some family history for me. "Your great-grandfather was a Jew, grew up on the Lower East Side, Jew Central. But he argued with his parents. It was the usual immigrant thing: assimilate but don't change, be American but speak Yiddish. So, he decided to go to California and work in the new movie racket. Jews seemed to run it. He learned how to edit film then changed his name and married a nice Midwestern girl from the chorus. They tied the knot it in a Methodist church and he never got around to telling her he was a Jew. Had been. Never saw his parents again. His brother took over the father's bathroom fixture business. Nice boy, but so dull."

"Did you live with all your descendants?"

"Live with? Like this, you mean? Nope. I looked in on a lot of them, sometimes for a day or two, a week, or just an hour-as a customer, a colleague, a neighbor. And, before you ask, never as a boyfriend or a spouse, God forbid. Oh, and never as a dog."

"So you had control of who and where you were?"

"I wish. It's called the World of Confusion for a reason."

I seized the chance to tell him about the fear that had been eating at me. "What if I'm the one who's in the Olam ha-Dimyon?"

"You? Impossible, Olivia. You're just a sweet mixed-up shiksa. Nobody called Olivia's going into this Hebrew purgatory. It's exclusive. Believe me."

"How can you be so sure?"

"When you're sure, you're sure."

I was about twenty-five percent comforted.

"Then you've never been an animal before?

"It's a whole new experience."

"Do you like it?"

"Well, it has its points. You live more in your body, more simply and purely. To tell the truth, it takes tremendous effort to think like a human, to speak sensibly. It feels unnatural; it goes against my instincts. Thinking like a dog's simple. Also, it's easier for a dog to be happy-at least for me. Just being near you does the trick, especially when you're not moping."

"I mope?"

He gave me that little canine shrug. "You're sixteen."

Hollering wafted up from the kitchen and I clutched at Baruch. "You're my real family," I said passionately.

But my impulsiveness made him cautious. "In a sense," he allowed, "but I'm still just a dog. Besides, I'm too far away in space and time. I'm an ancestor."

"What do you mean? You're right here, right now."

He shook his head at me. "It's not the same. Admit it."

I wouldn't. I just hugged Baruch closer. He licked my ear then shut up for five days.

7.

It was a fine Saturday afternoon and I had just put the last touches on my college essay. I disliked the thing but didn't hate it. The college essay is not so fine a genre as, say, the Petrarchan sonnet. To celebrate,

I took Baruch out for a long walk. We strolled all the way to Rheinach Park and sat down under my favorite copper beech.

He seemed subdued or maybe he was just worn out, going all that way on those four short legs.

We lay down on the grass. I put my hands behind my head and gazed up into the branches. "I used to climb up there," I said.

Baruch looked this way and that, making sure we were alone. Then he said, "I want to tell you a story."

"So, it's a talking day? Okay. Shoot."

"It's another one about the Olam. Alas, it's not exactly a happy one."

"Fine with me. I'm not exactly happy either. If I get in anywhere, I still have to wait months and months."

Baruch huffed glumly, as if to say, "You can't wait to get away from me? Do you wish I were really and truly dead?"

I patted his head. "Go on."

"We're back in the old country, you understand. It was a bitterly cold winter. A poor tailor whose wife had just given birth to a little girl gathered all the money he could find and went to the market to buy wood to warm them. Firewood was scarce that terrible winter, coal unheard-of. There were only a few sticks left and the tailor was about to buy them when a rich merchant stepped in front of him and offered the woodsman half again as much as the poor man could. The tailor begged the merchant to take pity on his wife and baby but, as they say, to no avail. Two days later both the wife and the child died of the cold. And two days after that, the tailor, broken-hearted and cold to the bone, also perished. Now, by coincidence, the very day the tailor died so did the rich merchant, overcome by a fit of apoplexy after being bested in a deal over some sable furs.

"Both men appeared before the Heavenly Court and the tailor lodged his complaint. The angels weren't at all surprised. They'd been keeping an eye on this merchant who had frequently been sued in earthly courts by people he cheated. But, since he could hire the cleverest lawyers, the merchant had always managed to get these suits referred to a higher court, one after the other until he finally found a judge who could be bribed to acquit him. The chief of the accusing angels read out all his sins, which took two days. A verdict was quickly arrived at. But the rich man, having died so suddenly and unexpectedly, was in the Olam ha-Dimyon and acted just as he would have had he still been alive. He insisted on appealing to a higher court. A panel of higher angels was duly summoned. They listened to the evidence and at once concurred with the verdict. 'I'll show you?!' shouted the rich merchant and declared he would appeal to an even higher court, 'to the emperor himself, if necessary!' This amused the angels who put their heads together then told the man that, if he wanted to appeal their judgment, he was free to do so."

"That's it? How does the story end?"

"That is the end. You see? He's still filing appeals."

I scratched Baruch behind his ears and thought about the story. "So, this means you're afraid you're being punished?"

"I was once convinced of it and for a long time I lived alone. I can't remember for how long. For a while I lived in the mountains, then under a bridge. Next, I built a little hut in the corner of a Jewish cemetery. Eventually I was driven out by the shammes. There was quite a jolly protest on my behalf by the children. I'd always thought they were scared of me. It was because of them that I was placed again among the living. At least I like to think so."

"Then maybe you aren't being punished at all. Maybe it's just some kind of mistake. Courts make them all the time."

"Not heavenly ones."

"Why not? They're so perfect?"

He turned his head and examined me. "Just then you sounded like. . ."

"Like what?"

"Like a Jew."

For some reason this made me laugh and I gave Baruch a kiss right on his wet black nose.

8.

Well, Miriam, I'm nearly finished. I've just changed your diaper. You smiled at me while I did it, so very sweetly, as if you were proud of what you'd produced and thought I was admiring it. I can't help wondering what you'll make of all this some day, if I decide to show it to you. I'm not entirely sure what I think of it myself. I've left out so much: my adolescent social life, for instance, the music I listened to constantly, the volleyball team, learning to drive in the parking lot of the Baptist church, trying pot (disliked it), wearing nothing but black (for about a month), the fifty ways I did my hair (don't ask). But this hasn't been about why my adolescence was difficult-everybody's is-it's the story of what helped me make it through. In that sense, there's a happy ending.

Four colleges accepted me. I chose the one furthest away. I loved being there, reveled in it even when I was depressed. Even as places to be miserable, colleges are better than high schools. I met your father my last year and that's a big part of the happy ending.

As you know, my parents did get divorced, though it took them another three years. Your father wasn't so patient. We're already separated. Happy? Unhappy? There's always a dot of ying in the yang and vice versa. On the day you were born, your father and I vowed we'd never divorce, that it would never happen to you. There will be no arguments over where the tomato paste belongs. And you won't have to wait sixteen years for some suave uncle to give you a puppy either. Still, who knows? A vow may just be an excess of exuberance, hope going overboard.

The summer before I left for school Baruch got out of the back yard. He ran into the street and was hit by a Jeep. The poor woman had three screaming kids in the Jeep and she was crying too and kept repeating, "I couldn't do anything. He just. . ." She meant that not only wasn't she responsible, but she wasn't guilty either, though guilt often hasn't much to do with responsibility. I've always believed this was Baruch's way of letting me off the hook, leaving me before I had to abandon him. He was, I hope, moving on. Father bore up manfully, but, to my surprise, Mother was devastated.

Was he being punished? Was I being rewarded? Was I a little mad? There are doctors who argue that adolescence is a form of madness. And there are rabbis who argue that the Olam ha-Dimyon, the World of Confusion, is this one, the one we're all in together. I guess it's as he said though, the dead can't be expected to know more about death than the living do about life.

On one point, though, I think Baruch was wrong. Miriam, my darling girl, though you're even less a Jew than I am, we all do our time in the World of Confusion.

THE STORY OF MY SOCIAL LIFE

The weighty envelope was addressed to me, that was certain, and yet I thought there had to be some mistake. Engraved with almost excessive elegance, the invitation looked and felt like solidified cream.

I had good reason to be astonished. Out of the blue, the pleasure of my company at a dinner party was being solicited, and the host was no less than the man whom I had admired above all others from the instant I first beheld his magnificent Cranmer Building. He was not only an architect of the first rank; his achievements encompassed civic and charitable as well as professional endeavors. As I learned from the newspaper, he moved with easy grace in circles so exalted that the thought of sitting down to a dinner over which he presided made my knees tremble.

I read my name on the envelope once more, each magic syllable, then plumped down on my desk chair. The invitation begged me to respond as soon as possible. A little card and stamped envelope, also engraved, had been inserted into the folded invitation for this purpose. Now there could be no doubt; above the boxes marked will attend and will not attend, beautifully hand-written in peacock blue ink, was my own name once again, and impeccably spelled.

Cold as it was that evening, I walked to Karlsholm's to get a drink, hoping to find Pym and Endicott there. The bar was fairly crowded with middle-aged men in business suits with ties askew, younger men in leather jackets or tweed sportscoats with open collars. My friends were not there, though. I ordered a beer, took a booth to myself, and began to reflect.

Perhaps I really ought not to have been so overwhelmed by the invitation, unexpected and unmerited though I felt it to be. Maybe I had failed to get over feeling myself still an immigrant, afflicted by the outsider's conviction of invisibility and keen sense of not belonging. After all, it had been nearly six years since I had arrived with my foreign degree and my ambition to build great houses, to make my name in stone and brick. Was it really so miraculous that my work, little though there was of it, should have attracted the attention of the great man? Since he was known to interest himself in everything, why not the efforts of a talented young colleague, one in whose work he would find echoes of his own? Wasn't it natural that such a magnanimous man should grant some recognition, lend a hand, want to meet in person a youthful admirer whose emulation his sharp eye would have quickly discerned? These congenial thoughts cheered me.

A quarter hour later, Pym bustled in on a gust of chilly air, his face all red beneath his ridiculous fur hat, his torso bent under the weight of his army surplus greatcoat, an extra-long scarf wrapped around his neck. He spotted me at once and came stiffly to the booth. "Jesus!" he managed to mouth. "It's damned near absolute zero out there."

"Yes. It's cold enough," I said. The truth was that I had barely noticed the cold myself.

Pym unwound his scarf. "I called Endicott, but that old woman claims he's sick and doesn't dare come out in this weather."

"Really? Anything serious?"

"Serious? You know he's a hopeless hypochondriac. Says it's flu, but he's probably just frightened of frostbite. He claims some uncle of his lost all his toes in the war or climbing a mountain or something. I'll bet he's told you the story more than once."

"Frostbite's no joke."

"Well, I need a whiskey," Pym declared and made for the bar.

Pym and Endicott were all but inseparable; they had been at college together. They befriended me not long after my arrival and it was to them I owed most of my initiation. Quite a pair they were, a study in contrasts. Pym was like a barrel with limbs, intrepid and careless about his language, his opinions, in his willingness to risk money and dignity. Slim Endicott was all prudence and circumspection, skeptical, a bit cheap and a little pedantic: a grasshopper and an ant. As often happens, it was the tension between their approaches to life that formed the foundation of their friendship. They took pleasure in upbraiding one another. Pym loved to accuse Endicott of cowardice and half-heartedness while Endicott was fond of forecasting financial and social ruin for his reckless friend. Toward women the two friends also held opposed attitudes. Pym flirted aggressively while Endicott blushed whenever a waitress so much as smiled at him. Long ago I determined that my best course lay in listening to the advice of both Pym and Endicott and then adopting a middle course.

I told Pym about the invitation. I would willingly have shown the card to him but hadn't dared to take the precious thing out of my room.

"Bravo! Fantastic!" he cried, his cheeks round and red. He hoisted his shot glass. "I see it all," he said gazing beatifically toward the ceiling. "Beautiful women with rich old husbands, rich old women with beautiful young husbands, caviar, champagne, a rack of lamb, three dinner wines, plus a sauterne with the dessert, and everybody curious about you, my boy. You'll wear a tuxedo, of course."

"A tuxedo?"

"Naturally."

"But you know I have only the one suit."

He clucked his tongue. "Not to worry. We'll rent you one."

"What?" I said. "Rent clothing?"

He laughed. "People do it all the time. Don't worry about a thing. I'll give you an address."

I had never heard of leasing clothing. It seemed indecent. "Is it expensive?" I asked.

"Oh, not very. And how are you intending to arrive? That's important, you know."

"Arrive?"

"How are you going to get there. You really ought to lease a limousine, but a cab will do."

Pym's extravagance on my behalf somehow reassured me so that by the time I left the bar I had begun to accustom myself to the idea of the dinner party and even a rented tuxedo.

I slept complacently that night. But the next day Endicott phoned. Pym had told him about my good fortune. Superficially, his view was no different from Pym's. He too saw the dinner invitation as a breakthrough, if not a triumph; but, even as he congratulated me, he warned me against overestimating the significance of the invitation.

"Has it occurred to you that this party is being given for quite a number of young people like yourself?"

Of course it hadn't occurred to me. Prompted by vanity and Pym, I had assumed that I would be the center of attention in a small gathering of accomplished, well-established people, the cream of society. I saw myself singled out as a rising star and, while Endicott may not have intended to throw cold water on my enthusiasm, he was a killjoy by nature and altered the way I pictured the party. I saw myself standing silently in a corner of the great man's spacious living room or seated at a long table between young men and women all of whom were far more talented and articulate than myself. I imagined my face frozen in a horrid rictus as sallies of wit flew over my head like mortar shells.

As I considered the shabbiness of my small apartment, my desk made out of a hollow door, my second-hand easy chair, my imitation

Persian carpet, I even regretted my hastiness in returning the little card committing myself to attend the party. After all, I thought defensively, isn't it my work that really matters? What have I, with my poverty and my accent, to do with tuxedos and beautiful women and sauterne?

The party was to take place the following Saturday night. The Wednesday before, I again met up with Pym at Karlsholm's. I had phoned Endicott to join us, but he begged off, insisting that he really did have the flu. Pym gave me the address of a place that rented evening clothes. Once again, his pleasure on my behalf raised my spirits. "And make sure they give you one that fits properly," he added with the sort of grin that says, "This is quite unnecessary, you old dog."

I went to the shop the next morning. To my surprise, after one appraising look, the proprietor pulled out a jet-black tuxedo and asked me to slip on the jacket. It fit perfectly, better than the jacket to my own suit, in fact better than any jacket I'd ever worn. I tried on two pairs of trousers and the second was just right. In the whole outfit, I looked quite elegant. Though a little staggered by the rental price, I agreed, and arranged to pick the tuxedo up Saturday morning. I left the shop and went directly to my bank to draw out some cash. The tuxedo and the cab required more money than I could spare. Not only would there be no more beers for the rest of the month, but I'd have to economize on food as well. My two part-time jobs-junior architect and contract draftsman-may have brought me to the attention of my idol, but they did not bring in much money.

I recollected Pym's advice. "It's always wise to invest in decent vestments, old chum."

At ten o'clock on a leaden Saturday, I went to pick up the tuxedo. The proprietor was not there. Instead, a young woman sat reading a paperback novel and chewing gum. She asked for my name twice, frowned, checked the book on the counter, then looked at me suspiciously.

My stomach fell. "Is there a problem?"

"Could you just say that name again for me? I mean, really really slow?"

"Maybe I should spell it for you. Would that help? It's not very common."

But even correctly spelled my name did not appear in her ledger. I began to panic.

"Perhaps you could telephone the proprietor?"

"He's in the hospital," she reported without showing any sympathy for either him or me. "Heart attack."

As the young woman seemed to consider the matter settled, she went back to her novel and her rumination. I beseeched her to see if my tuxedo might not be in one of the plastic bags hanging on the rack behind her.

She sighed and put down her book. "Oh, all right," she whined and began yanking the suits along the rack so that they screeched. "Nope," she said.

Casting all restraint to the winds I pleaded with her. "But I have to have that tuxedo by tonight. You don't know what depends on it!"

She looked at me blankly. "You getting married or something?"

"Look," I said more calmly, "have you got any tuxedos in the back that aren't reserved?"

"Look, mister, I just keep the cash register."

I implored her just to take one look, to indulge me.

She put her hands on her hips. "I can't just leave the register, can I? I mean I'm all alone here, aren't I?"

"Good Lord, then I'll leave for five minutes. Would that be all right? You can lock the door behind me."

"Oh sure. And what if another customer shows up?"

"I'll wait outside, all right? You lock the door. If somebody else comes to the shop, I'll explain everything and make him wait."

To my surprise, she agreed to this absurd proposal and so I stood in the cold wind just outside the door until, still chewing ferociously, she let me back in.

On the counter lay two tuxedos, neither in a plastic bag.

"Here," she said with exasperation. "I guess you can have either of these."

I looked at the suits. The jacket of one was soiled with food stains while the other was at least two sizes too large.

I took the large one, tossing my cash down on the counter, threw the suit over my shoulder and headed for the door.

"Hey, just a minute," she said and took a frilled shirt, bow tie, and a little bag of studs from under the counter. "You're going to need these. And when you bring it back make sure the tie's in the jacket pocket. Bring it back on Monday, but not before noon."

By now I was not only in a temper but convinced that the evening was certain to be a catastrophe. How could I get through it with any dignity swimming in a tuxedo fit for the heavyweight champion? I thought how Pym would chuckle if he were to see me in this outfit, then how he would hasten to reassure me that I looked decidedly debonair. "A real lady-killer, old chum," he'd have said, good old Pym. Not without envy, I pictured Endicott snug in his bed, nursing himself on bouillon, thanking his flu that he at least didn't have to go out to a dinner party in such frigid weather.

I put the tuxedo on as soon as I got home. While not even Pym in his cups could have called it a good fit, at least I didn't look entirely grotesque. I was fortunate to have a pair of good black shoes. I had bought them at home, for funerals, and wore them only during the first week after my arrival. They were reasonably presentable. I dragged my desk chair in the bathroom and, from what I was able to see in the small mirror over the sink, I certainly wouldn't appear to such advantage as I hoped, but also not so ridiculous as I feared. Nevertheless, when the time came to call for a cab, my dread returned. The sky had lowered to just above the rooftops. I worried that the cab would be late or that, like the tuxedo shop, the taxi company might accept my call and then simply forget about it. I didn't live in the sort of neighborhood where people could hail cabs on the street.

So, I was relieved when, at the precise time I had stipulated, a cab pulled up outside and honked its horn. Being careful to place my invitation in the breast pocket of the tuxedo, I threw on my carefully brushed overcoat and dashed down the stairs.

A sheet of heavy plastic separated me from the driver who wore a cap pulled low over his forehead and grunted when I read him the address from my invitation. It wasn't easy to extract it from my pocket, but I didn't dare trust memory.

We were off at once. The driver proceeded with such dispatch and assurance through the narrow streets of my neighborhood that I finally stopped leaning forward, sank back into the seat, and gave myself up to the luxurious sensation of being driven.

"How long will it take to get there?" I asked almost nonchalantly.

When the driver didn't reply, I assumed he couldn't hear me over the engine noise and through the protective shield. I smiled at myself, looked out the window, and tried to relax.

We made our way through the thickening dusk toward the river. The streetlamps came on and in their yellow aura I could see that a light snow had begun to fall. As we shot across the bridge, I started to worry that I might arrive too soon. How humiliating to be the first guest! The invitation said six-thirty, but maybe it would be unfashionable to show up before seven or even seven-thirty. I cursed myself for not having consulted Pym and Endicott on such an essential point.

By the time we had crossed the bridge night had fallen and I noticed that the driver now seemed less sure of where he was going. Not only did we move more slowly, but, from time to time, he pulled up at corners, as though he were checking street signs. The snow began to fall in earnest and the cab's wipers could barely keep the windshield clear. No doubt the roads were slippery too.

So, we drove slowly on, making many turns. Whenever we passed directly beneath a streetlamp, I checked my watch. It was growing late. It was past six-thirty already.

"Look, driver," I said loudly, leaning up against the plastic shield, "are you lost?"

A muffled sound came from the front and we pulled over to the curb. The driver turned around and I saw terror in his eyes.

"What is it?"

"No report," he pleaded in a high-pitched voice, a voice from some forsaken desert or mountain. "No report. Please. Wife. Two baby. No report, please. I lose job. Two baby. Please!"

I grasped it all at once. An immigrant like myself, lost among the tended boulevards of the wealthy, he hadn't dared to turn down a fare. No doubt he had tried to bluff it out, hoping for the best. Oh, I understood the poor fellow only too well.

"You're lost," I couldn't help saying a little angrily, not so much to reproach him as to make my doom more certain.

He quickly turned off the meter. "Look, look," he said with a depressing attempt at ingratiation. "No charge, no charge."

"Maybe we can get directions somewhere," I suggested, looking hopelessly around at the solid mansions looming through large snowflakes that were falling like hunks of metal.

"I try again," he said desperately.

And so, we pushed on through still streets. Twice I thought of asking him to take me home but told myself that, after all, it was not so terribly late, especially not if it were fashionable to arrive a later than requested. I might even still be early.

I ordered the driver to pull up in front of a well-lit house.

"I'm going to ask there," I said as slowly and clearly as I could, remembering how people used to substitute volume for distinctness when I had not understood them. "You wait. Understand? You wait."

He nodded and I clambered out.

As I was ringing the bell I heard the cab pull away. He did it slowly, stealthily. Perhaps the poor man was too frightened to bear any more, or maybe he had misunderstood me and thought that this was where I had wanted to go.

According to the manservant who answered the door, I was only a mile from my destination. I could hear people talking and laughing inside. The mistress of the house came to see what was the matter-a heavy, imposing woman in a green silk dress and long, flashing earrings. I was interrupting her party, it seemed. With some annoyance, my tuxedo and my engraved invitation notwithstanding, she brusquely rattled off a complicated set of directions, turned away, and ordered the servant to shut the door.

Twice I lost my way. My shoes were soon sodden, my hands numb. My nose ran like a melting icicle, and my stomach growled, demanding to know what had become of the promised caviar and rack of lamb. Mesmerized by the falling snow, I walked among the grand houses, wishing I had a hat. Careless of my being an architect, the houses did not put themselves out to be friendly; they stood upright and aloof on either side of me like the inaccessible pillars of society who owned them.

At last, I succeeded in finding the correct avenue. I halted under the street sign to check my watch and wipe my nose on my sleeve. How late it had gotten-far too late even to be fashionable! Shouldn't I just give up and make my way back to the river? A cab might be found waiting by the bridge; it could whisk me home to my desk and my worn rug, to my dear narrow bed on which I could stretch out and forget everything. But then I remembered the honor done me by my host, my admiration for him. I stiffened my resolve. Even if I should now be too late for dinner, I could not insult the great man by not at least putting in an appearance. I imagined myself greeted with cries of sympathy, installed by a fireplace, surrounded by well dressed people who were relieved to see me and who attended sympathetically to the story of my difficulties. Somehow, I would contrive to make the dreary tale light and diverting, and they would all laugh while my host, smiling at my tale, personally fetched me a snifter of cognac.

It took me ten more minutes to locate the house. As there was no light over it, I found the number with difficulty. It was a dignified neo-classical villa in the French style fronted by a balustrade on which the snow had formed little sugary arches. The number matched the one on my invitation and yet the place was completely dark. I was puzzled. Warm, festive light should be pouring over the new snow from its long windows. Ah, I thought, they've just pulled the curtains to make it all the cozier inside.

I marched up the front steps and crossed a small portico to the door. I listened for laughter and chamber music but could hear nothing at all. What solid construction, I thought appreciatively. I took off my glove and blew on my frozen hand, then rang the bell. I had to wait quite a while and twice more wiped my nose on my coat sleeve, fearful that the door might open in mid-wipe. They're having such a time in there that they haven't heard the bell, I told myself, and gave another ring-a good long one this time.

Finally, the door opened. There stood my host himself, but-and this quite paralyzed me-in pajamas, robe, and slippers. Just as he opened the door, before he had a chance to say a word, a woman's frightened voice called out from within, "Who is it, Alfred?"

"Just a minute," said my host with irritation, though whether to me or the woman I couldn't tell. He disappeared for an instant and the portico light came on.

"Oh," he said, "it's you. Did you forget something?"

"Forget something?"

The great architect, my idol, rubbed his balding head and pulled his robe tight against the cold. "Look, it's rather late. I don't know why you've come back, but you can see it's not convenient." His controlled fury left me as speechless as when I had first arrived in this country, wearing my black shoes and hardly understanding the language, before I had met Pym and Endicott and found my footing. "Please be so good as to go home now," he added and shut the door.

I walked through the snow not even wondering whether I was making for the river. Almost the worst of it was knowing that when I told Pym and Endicott about this fiasco-and I would have to tell them, they were my only friends-they would argue about it, elaborating complicated views that canceled each other out.

THYSSEN-PORLOCK DISEASE

Patient: van Ruys, Cassandra

Age: 28

Diagnosis: T-P

Notes: Patient was diagnosed during a trip to visit her family in the south of France. She was fortunate to be seen by Dr. Alexandre Sartout, with whom I have exchanged emails about my research on two occasions. When Dr. Sartout determined that his patient would be returning here, he remembered our exchanges and referred her to me.

Patient presents with T-P symptoms including bouts of ataxia, intermittent fevers, some weakness in all four limbs, and repeated lung infections. Her bp is moderately low.

Medical history: unexceptional until age 24. Her mother and grandmother died at 43 and 49, respectively, cause of both deaths recorded as pneumonia but most likely T-P.

Prognosis: poor.

Proposed treatment: my latest gene-silencing formula.

Additional background and observations: Patient works as an assistant textbook manager in the University's bookstore. Has considerable resources owing to a generous allowance from her father, a retired maritime insurance executive. Shortly after her mother's death, her father remarried, has a new family, seldom sees patient. The fortunate visit that led her to Dr. Sartout was their first personal contact in five years. Some of this information was in Sartout's file. When I asked the patient follow-up questions, she answered willingly and clearly. Patient shows some anxiety, is articulate, soft-spoken, intelligent, blonde-haired, blue-eyed with delicate features. Patient is exceptionally beautiful.

At our first appointment, Cassandra reported having just gotten over a month-long bout of bronchitis. When I asked about her general condition, she answered cheerfully.

"I'm feeling well, at least by contrast to how I was feeling two weeks ago."

The emotional response this answer provoked in me was a surprise. I felt happy but, at the same time, melancholy.

Cassandra was familiar with her disease in so far as a layperson could be, having consulted the usual online sources since returning from France. There was not much I could tell her about Thyssen-Porlock. She knew it was hereditary and her prospects. I explained the new practice of gene-silencing and that this is what I wanted to do for her, that the treatment was experimental, expensive, and might have side-effects I couldn't predict.

"The money won't be a problem," she said dryly, "but I guess neither of us can say whether the side-effects will be," she added with a smile.

My chest ached.

As a consequence of losing her mother, Cassandra lost her father as well, though in a different way. My impression was that Mr. van Ruys had substituted money for love or, at the least, attention. Perhaps, as an insurance man, he knew the flaw in that formula, that the price of replacing a ship is not the same as the ship. Yet I'm convinced this is what he did, giving what he had plenty of instead of what he wasn't prepared to spare. I didn't blame him. His daughter had come here to attend the university long before and stayed on. The man had a new life, new wife, new child. His retirement, which she told me coincided with his second marriage, suggested van Ruys had drawn a line firmly dividing his old life from the new. Maybe Cassandra saw things this way, too. On the few occasions when she mentioned her father, it was without resentment. I never heard a bad word from her about either him or his new wife. She spoke only of her father's generosity and her gratitude. My fee was paid promptly and without complaint.

I was not a brilliant medical student. I briefly thought of becoming a surgeon but knew I lacked both the talent and the courage. I recoiled from a dull future as, at best, a mediocre general practitioner. So, I conceived the idea of specializing in some condition so rare that I would be, so to speak, instantly distinguished as an expert owing to the scarcity of competitors. "Specialist," I figured, is a title with which you can't go wrong. It has an aura of authority and inspires confidence, even though it has no practical significance.

I reviewed hundreds of diseases and syndromes in the medical library, a demoralizing and unsettling pursuit. Before long, I wondered that anybody is alive at all. I stopped when I happened on Thyssen-Porlock, only recently established as an incurable hereditary disease. I liked the name but also that so little was known about it. I could quickly learn as much as anybody. It also was appealing that I would know more about the disorder than my professors.

Shortly after I completed my internship, I married Teresa Vananzi, a newly qualified ICU nurse. We'd stared at each other for a week in the corridors and the cafeteria before I asked her out. Banks are generous with doctors, even newly qualified ones. I borrowed the money for a little house in the suburbs. As a married man with a mortgage, I needed a steady income. Laying aside my plan to specialize, I spent three years as an emergency room physician. The work was hard, the hours terrible, the effect demoralizing. That third year, at the hospital's Christmas party for staff and their families, Teresa was introduced to a celebrated heart surgeon. Four months later she left me.

We divorced. The house was sold. There were no children, a minimum of property to be divided. Eventually, my mother stopped weeping during our Sunday and Wednesday phone calls, and I was free to return to my original plan.

Specialists in obscure ailments charge colossal fees. The expense gives most patients confidence, especially if they've plenty of money. My fee was high too, and yet my income was less than a newly qualified general practitioner's. Why? First, I had few patients because Thyssen-Porlock is rare and seldom diagnosed. Moreover, the price of the drugs I required for my experiments was staggering. My fee had to cover those, keep me fed, my old Civic gassed, and supply the rent and utility bills for the first-floor apartment which served both as home and clinic. The few poor T-P patients who made their way to me I treated on a "sliding scale"-that is, gratis. I saw a few regular patients to eke things out and spent two days a week at a free clinic because I had time on my hands and enjoyed the work. It made me feel useful and I met interesting people. My colleagues assumed that, because I was a specialist, I had to be rich and, as they knew of no one else who treated Thyssen-Porlock, even richer than they were. I was surprised then amused by the unmerited respect this earned me at the few professional gatherings I attended.

My neighborhood was neither the worst nor the best in the city, though nearer the former than the latter. It was working-class with a mixture of young families crowded into duplexes and elderly people, not yet shunted into care facilities and who lacked the money or inclination to move south. My next-door neighbors were old Mrs. O'Donnell and still older Mrs. Ardekian. They liked to check out my patients. Who came in a big SUV, who on foot? How were they dressed? They approved of the variety of my clientele and were further pleased when they learned about my work at the free clinic. Consequently, I sometimes got casseroles and cookies. In return, I was consulted about coughs, sores, aches. In short, I was accepted and respected. It wasn't a bad life, though a lonely one.

I had been working on my gene-silencing treatment for four years, helped by a small grant from a foundation dedicated to rare diseases. The first year went on basic research, the second on experimentation after I secured approval to experiment with RNAi on human subjects who were otherwise untreatable. For my work, I required DNA and RNA from T-P sufferers. I obtained samples from two patients I had treated with palliative therapies, the best I could do for them. Both were terribly ill yet neither reproached me. In fact, they were generous, eager to help. At considerable cost, I obtained five more samples from a private laboratory in Denmark. The company had begun then abandoned research on T-P as unlikely to be profitable. My experiments focused on finding out how to turn off the evil messages in the RNA. By then, I thought of my work not just scientifically, with detachment, but also morally, with passion.

I tried different combinations of drugs and one showed real promise in three of the Danish samples. This was the formula I first tried on Cassandra. She had come to me in springtime. I initially scheduled her for four treatments, one a week between April and May.

"I like coming here," she said at our third session. She was sitting on the examination table, her legs dangling like a child's. By then, it was all I could do to conceal how much I looked forward to her visits. "You're a kind man and, of course, you give me hope. I'm grateful to Dr. Sartout for sending me to you."

Cassandra took a folded tissue from her breast pocket and rubbed her nose. She was getting over a cold. How that cold had terrified me.

I always asked the usual questions but added some less clinical ones each week. Doesn't love begin with curiosity, the urge to know, to penetrate? Isn't love a kind of tender aggression?

"What was your major?"

"Don't make fun of me."

"Why would I do that?"

"People do," she said a little abashed, lowering her head. "My degree's in French literature. Totally impractical."

"Not if you live in France," I said.

"Or Belgium."

I smiled encouragingly.

"Or Québec."

"Oui, oui, Québec. Je me souviens."

"You speak French?"

"It's on the license plates."

"Ha!"

"You have favorite writers?"

She brightened. "Oh, so many! Gide, Camus, Duras, Colette, Baudelaire, Rimbaud, Hugo, Giraudoux, Valéry. Did you know it was by translating Balzac that Dostoyevsky taught himself to write novels?"

"I'm a humble monolingual physician. It's news to me, though I've read The Idiot. In translation, of course."

It wasn't hard to make Cassandra smile; nevertheless, I worked at it, given the reward. She was-in effect-an orphan. Like her female forbears, she might be doomed to an early death. And neither of us could forget that.

Cassandra showed no improvement. I tried to think of ways to change the medication. I would wake up in the middle of the night, scribble down ideas, throw them away in the morning.

What else did I do? Most evenings I watched movies. My mother had given me a subscription to Netflix as a birthday present. "So your nights will be less lonely," she said rather spitefully. In other words, I was pathetic, to be pitied and mortified. The subtext was And where are my grandchildren? But I did watch a lot of films. That spring I began to work my way through the French New Wave, inspired by Cassandra's undergraduate major. The films I'd seen a decade before and thought mannered and pretentious now struck me as liberating, full of light and charm. I was taken with their pacing, levity, spontaneity, the absence of anything ponderous or formulaic.

It was after watching one of Truffaut's films that the idea popped in my head for a change to Cassandra's medication, a slight adjustment that, perhaps because of how it had come to me, I thought promising. What is inspiration anyway but finding without looking-or after you've given up looking?

On her third visit, Cassandra was accompanied by another young woman, a more robust one. She was supporting Cassandra with an arm around her waist.

"My best friend," said Cassandra in a weak, winded voice.

"Marina Sokolovsky," said the other, holding out her hand for me to shake. Her grip was so strong it seemed almost a challenge. She looked me in the face frankly, appraisingly.

I don't believe it was because Marina rhymes with Karina that she seemed to me so much like the heroine and muse of so many of Jean-Luc Godard's films. She had the same dark bangs, memorable eyes, soft lips, the same lively mobility of expression. When, later, I had more opportunity to observe her, I learned that Marina could change from almost schoolgirlish to schoolmarmishly severe in a moment.

She was obviously anxious about her friend, just like me. While she waited in my living room, I took Cassandra into my office, examined her, then explained what I wanted to do and why.

"It's experimental," I cautioned, "but no riskier than what we've been doing. It's all been experimental."

"Okay, then," she said bravely in her weakened soprano. "Let's go on experimenting."

Mentally crossing my fingers, I administered the new formula.

The following night I got a phone call from Marina Sokolovsky. She asked if it would be possible to see me. I was scheduled to be at the free clinic the next day until four-thirty. I asked if she would like to meet at my house at five.

"I'll be there."

She was waiting by the door when I got home, though it was not yet five.

I asked her in and we settled down in the living room. She was edgy, clasping and unclasping her hands, fiddling with a loose thread on the armrest.

"I asked to see you to talk about Cassie, of course. Confidentially. I'd be grateful if you kept this between us."

I didn't reply.

"Look, I understand that you can't discuss her case with me, at least not the particulars. But I know about Thyssen-Porlock. I've read everything I could find, including your article on the danger of lung infections."

"I can see you're worried about your friend. I am, too."

To this Marina made no reply.

"She's not just a patient to me."

"Good. I want to know that you're doing everything you can. Also, I wanted to know if there's anything I can do."

"You watch over her?"

She shrugged. "It may not be the ideal way of putting it, but yes." She smiled.

"You know what I'm trying to do?"

She nodded. "Gene-silencing."

"I have hopes."

"But she's not improving and she's so pale and weak. And she's losing weight. I'm terrified that she'll catch something."

"So am I."

I had been working flat out at the clinic since ten that morning and I was hungry. Also, if I'm completely honest, I wasn't ready to part with Marina Sokolovsky.

I checked my watch, "Look," I said, "I haven't eaten since breakfast. There's a decent diner two blocks away. Would you join me for an early dinner?"

Marina didn't recoil, but she did pull her head back just an inch or two and eyed me with a moue very much like one of Anna Karina's.

"Why not?"

I could almost hear a pouting Anna saying, "Pourquoi pas?"

It was too early for the diner to be crowded. We took a booth. I ordered meat loaf. Astonishing that I can still remember what Marina had. She ordered a cheese omelet and a salad. "Something light," she said.

Marina confirmed my guess about Cassandra's relationship with her father and told me that she didn't care for her stepmother. She talked about her friend's grief for her mother and how her illness had stymied her.

"She's afraid to change anything. I mean, it's as if she's paralyzed. That's why she stays on at the bookstore when she could do so much more. She doesn't even like it there."

I asked Marina what she was doing.

"Oh me? I'm a grad student. Cassie and I met at the bookstore."

"What are you working on? I mean, what's your field?"

"Computational social science, a new discipline. Fairly new, anyway."

"It sounds interesting."

She scoffed. "Interesting's what people say when they're not interested. But it interests me."

"No, I 'd really like to know. What exactly is computational. . . social science?" I came within a Freudian hair of saying sociable silence.

"It's the use of data aggregation to uncover previously undetectable patterns of behavior in large groups. That would be the official definition."

"Isn't a lot of that sort of data confidential? Private?"

My naiveté made her grin. I thought she was going to say, "So you still think there's such a thing as privacy?" But she didn't.

"We never identify individuals, of course. Aggregated data without personal identities can, in most instances, be shared legally. Besides, I work for the government. That helps get cooperation."

"That sounds a bit chilling."

Marina had a contralto laugh, half an octave lower than Cassandra's soprano.

"I was kidding. Well, not entirely. I've got a government grant for my research."

"From DOD? CIA?"

She laughed again.

"No. Nothing so sinister. The grant's from the NSF's Sociology Program. I'm working on patterns of segregation and integration in neighborhoods and schools-also food distribution."

"So. . . real estate?"

"It's a bit more complicated."

"Real estate, red-lining, race and class?"

"You like teasing people, don't you?"

"It's the default position of the excruciatingly shy."

"You have a sense of humor."

"You mean, at least?"

"Do you tease Cassie?"

I shook my head. It never occurred to me to tease Cassandra. She was a patient; she was ill.

Marina's intelligence and vitality were as attractive as her face, and I liked making her laugh. It was a challenge; I could tell that she didn't often do it. Sure enough, the smile suddenly vanished and her expression turned serious, nearly menacing.

"Can you cure Cassie or not?"

I was taken aback.

"It's a simple binary. Yes or no."

"I don't know."

"Have you cured anyone?"

"One patient. I think."

"You think?"

"Too soon to be sure."

With one hand she made a fist; with the other she tugged at her sweater.

"Has anybody ever cured anyone with T-P-for sure?"

"You've done your homework, so you know the answer."

Marina lifted her shoulders and sighed.

"Well, you're honest."

"At least?"

"Hmph."

"I have hopes, Marina. High ones. Really."

She fixed me with a hard look, narrowed her eyes and pointed a finger.

"You'd better."

Marina Sokolovsky infiltrated my dreams. She appeared as a prosecutor, a teacher, a nightclub singer. I never dreamed about Cassandra. I resolved to take myself in hand, to be more detached, and to watch fewer films like Two English Girls.

The adjusted medication achieved quick results, astonishing ones. By the fourth week it felt like a breakthrough. I foresaw an article in JAMA or The Lancet. But what was that beside saving the exquisite Cassandra and earning the gratitude of the fascinating Marina?

I decided to add a fifth treatment. Cassandra and Marina both came. The latter was holding a big potted plant with lots of yellowish green leaves. They were in a jolly mood. Marina giggled when she told me they'd gone on a three-mile hike the previous Sunday.

Cassandra grinned. "I could have gone for another two miles," she said smugly.

Marina pushed the plant into my arms. "Something living for your living room."

"It's a Golden Dieffenbachia," said Cassandra, just like a child proud of being able to pronounce the name.

She looked radiant. Both did.

I took Cassandra into the office. The first thing I did was weigh her.

"You've put on weight. Almost five pounds."

"I've got the appetite of a lumberjack."

I gave Cassandra a thorough going over before administering the final dose. What I found was exciting. Her blood pressure was at the low end of the normal range, and her lungs were perfectly clear.

It was over.

At the door, I said, "You'll come back in a month and let me check how you're doing?"

"Of course," said Cassandra. "In a month."

"I can't tell you how grateful," mumbled Marina, as if embarrassed.

They both gave me a peck on the cheek and took each other by the hand on the way out.

That's when I knew that they loved each other and that neither would ever love me.

OSTBRÜCK

Only two weeks after the old Count died leaving no heir, his only son having been killed in the war that placed Friedrich-Wolfgang in the Electorship, armed men from the adjacent baronies of Dalhausen and Metz-Hagenau invaded Ostbrück. They tore up fields, plundered four villages, killed a score of peasants, and raped a dozen women before skirmishing with each other outside the walled market town of Benehmen. After this indecisive engagement both detachments withdrew over Ostbrück's eastern and western frontiers, respectively. The two barons, each intent on annexing Ostbrück and still more on denying it to his rival, at once set about raising more troops and preparing for full-scale war.

Three days later, the Count's widow, accompanied by a delegation of Ostbrück's nobles and leading merchants, traveled to the Elector's palace to plead for his intervention. The Elector welcomed them courteously, found them accommodations, ordered a feast, at which he seated the Countess on his right. He approved the look of the nobles and the manners of the merchants of Ostbrück and would very much have relished conversing with the latter. It was to their credit when they bowed and declared that the good lady Countess would be speaking for them. Friedrich-Wolfgang was drawn to merchants, notwithstanding their low birth. Ostbrück, a city-state far smaller than its neighbors, had made itself into a prosperous mercantile center. The Elector had esteemed the old Count for encouraging these developments and, like him, found men of business clever and curious, both well-traveled and often surprisingly well read. The truth was that he preferred the company of a glove-maker or dealer in spices to men like the barons who had designs on Ostbrück.

The Elector attended to all the Countess had to say on behalf of her people who, according to her, were about to be torn to pieces by two arrogant wolves, both of whom had long cast a covetous eye on Ostbrück. "They were only waiting for my husband to die," she said, then added pointedly, "knowing he had no heir."

The Elector felt distressed. He had little respect and no affection for the Barons Dalhausen and Metz-Hagenau. Though one was scarcely thirty and the other nearly sixty, they were much alike: haughty, reactionary, petty, egotistical, greedy, hedonistic, brutal, and not excessively encumbered with intelligence-in short, typical of the nobility. During the struggle over the Electorship both had remained neutral not out of cowardice but simply because each was waiting for the other to declare himself in order to take the opposing side. In contrast, the Count's only heir had perished in the service of the future Elector.

The Elector would have liked to protect Ostbrück but did not see how he could do so. He explained to the Countess that her plea had moved him, and he dearly wished to assist her and her industrious and worthy people. However, his own army of vassals having been decimated by the war of succession, he found himself dependent on the nobles for troops and money. In fact, at the present time, he found himself little more than a figurehead with more responsibility than power. The latter came from ownership of land and that was in the hands of the barons and dukes, many of whom, he pointed out, had so recently been his enemies.

The Countess's reply was blunt. "That's politics," she said sternly. "My appeal is to honor."

Red-faced, Friedrich said he would do what he could and, rising from the table, ended the conversation and the banquet.

The Elector was not fond of his wife, their marriage having been arranged by his ambitious father when Friedrich-Wolfgang was only twelve. Margaret did not much care for her husband either, but she was enthralled with his new position and her title of Electress. At the banquet, Friedrich had observed with disgust as she made no effort to keep up with the lively talk of the merchants but looked down her nose at them, dropping names and titles like rose petals to strew her own path. "When I last stayed with Herman, the Duke of Thuringia. . . The Emperor himself confided to me that. . . that new Bohemian queen is not half so beautiful as people say. . ."

The woman Friedrich loved was named Franziska, whom he had installed in a modest mansion a half hour's walk from the palace. There was no secret about their relationship but, he felt, propriety required that half-hour.

Unlike Margaret, who was at once snobbish and bovine, Franziska was passionate, lovely, and possessed of more brains than his consort and all her ladies-in-waiting put together. Such a high regard did the Elector have for his mistress that he would often seek her advice, which was always sound and delivered in her own style.

When Franziska was twelve, the same age as the Elector when his father married him off, a squadron of mounted knights murdered her father, a horse dealer, raped her and carried off both her and the horses, leaving the family homestead in flames. Seeing that his lord, a margrave, admired her exceptional beauty, the captain of these knights sold her to him for fifty acres of barley and woodland. The margrave soon wearied of using a woman who would not give her consent, and so made of her a present to the Duke of Mainz. At Mainz she lived as a miserable ornament of the court for two years until the visit of the newly installed Elector. Friedrich did not look at her as these other men had. He sought her out and talked with her almost as an equal, and as a man who is not happy. Franziska believed she had steeled her heart with hatred of the high and mighty and was astonished to find herself attracted to the young Elector. As for Friedrich, he was wholly enchanted. Matters were soon arranged with the Duke, helped along by a timely reminder from the Elector that the Duke had been less than whole-hearted in support of his cause when it counted most.

Franziska felt that her hatred of the nobility found some echo in the Elector. How else could she have fallen in love with him? How else could she have felt joy when he took her with him from Mainz?

When Friedrich came to her that evening after the banquet, weighed down by his problem with Ostbrück, her far-seeing mind glimpsed an immense prospect, a vast landscape illuminated as if by a lightning flash. Her heart beat as fast as it had when Friedrich had first taken her in his arms.

"Have you ever seen two boys who've found some silver?" she asked him.

"What do you mean?"

"Say they're lucky enough to discover a fallen purse."

"They'd fight over it."

"I think they would. Now say that instead of two boys there are three."

"Three?"

"Would they fight over it too?"

"They might."

"Perhaps, but would you say it was more or less likely?"

"Less."

"Then three may share what two will fight over?"

"Yes, I suppose so."

Franziska drew the Elector toward her wide bed.

"How many barons want to seize Ostbrück?"

"Two. Dalhausen and Metz-Hagenau."

"And, in your opinion, these two are about to fight, even if you were to propose a fair division of Ostbrück between them?"

"Undoubtedly. I know those greedy men only too well."

"What if you gave all of the land to one of them?"

"That would be still worse. The other would be bitter. I'd make an enemy of him; there would be war anyway, and my authority would be undermined."

"It's certainly a dilemma. And what if there were a third?"

"They still might fight. Besides, the Ostbrückers aren't longing to be oppressed, and, anyway, there is no third claimant."

"One can't be found?"

"What?"

"Well, suppose this third were more powerful than either of the two barons, stronger even than both of them banded together. What then?"

"Even if there were such a one, slicing the place into thirds would still cost the people the advantages of their independence. Thanks to the old Count, Ostbrück is an oasis of trade in an ocean of rye and beets. I fear that won't remain so if they're devoured, whether there should be one diner, two, or three."

"Yes, I see that. But what if you were to put conditions on the division of Ostbrück?"

"Conditions?"

"Conditions that not only ensured the survival of Ostbrück's trade but caused it to flourish. What if the nobles could be made to see a benefit to themselves in promoting trade instead of frustrating it, as they do now?"

"Take down the tollgates, you mean?"

"I think that would be a good start, My Lord, don't you?"

Franziska lay down on the bed.

"Wait," said the Elector, "those two boys who are joined by a third? The ones with the purse?"

"Yes?"

"They'll be angry at not getting all the silver for themselves."

"Disappointed, yes, but neither would be embittered. Isn't one handful of silver better than a dagger in the gut and no silver at all?"

The Elector considered this while Franziska began to undress. Pulling her chemise over her head, she asked, "If there were a third, would it be better for Ostbrück if he were nearby or far off?"

"If he were nearby and as powerful as you say, he'd be sure to go to war."

"Then let him be far off. Do you think such a great noble might be capable of seeing that what he can collect in tariffs and taxes on trade will greatly exceed what he could get from, from turnips and oats?"

"Possibly. But what of poor Ostbrück?"

"My Lord, let's suppose that three tall men armed with quarterstaffs attack a short one, but the short one is a trained and armored knight on a warhorse. Who would win, the three tall or the one short man?"

The Elector stroked his beard and admired Franziska as she lay back on the bed.

"I think I see."

Franziska drew herself up, pressed her breasts against the Elector's chest, and gave him a warm kiss. In his ear she whispered, "I haven't studied maps, but I believe Franconia is leagues and leagues away from Ostbrück, isn't it?"

"The Franconian duke is rich and powerful. And he would be grateful."

"To you. Yes."

Franziska lay back on the feather bed and fetchingly bent one shapely leg.

"Tell me, Your Highness, why is it that the Elector is at once so high and yet so weak?"

"Because of the nobles, who own the land."

"Yet you admitted there's more wealth to be had from trade than land, no?"

"Potentially, yes."

"Well then, suppose trade in all of your domain begins to flourish. Who then will have the most wealth?"

"The merchants."

"And will these merchants want tolls every two leagues, new weights and measures every five, roads infested with robbers, and no navy to protect their argosies?" She put her hands on either side of the Elector's head and gently drew him to her. "Will they endure being lorded over by petty lords and Junkers? What do you think, will those merchants desire a powerful central government or a weak one?"

"They would need a strong one, of course, much stronger than mine."

Franziska rubbed Friedrich's temples. "Tell me, as Elector, what is it you have and what you lack?"

"I have authority but no money."

"And those merchants, should they flourish? What would they have and what would they lack?"

Friedrich laughed at her cleverness and the curious way she had of showing it. "They would have money but no authority."

Franziska smiled slyly. "With whom, then, would such men naturally ally themselves, and against whom?"

When the Elector left her at dawn, Franziska gave herself up to imagining the future she hoped she had set in motion. It might take longer than her lifetime to come to pass, yet she could see it plainly, how, for a time, Ostbrück would appear to have been betrayed, how the Elector would be cursed for its dismemberment. But if Friedrich did as she advised then Ostbrück would prosper and therefore be emulated. She had seen the way to her revenge at last, how in the end Ostbrück's prosperity would bring about the destruction of the nobility.

ROPE-MAKER

When Philippe summoned me to his office, I figured I was in hot water over my last feature. Perhaps the Minister of Education had complained about my choice of adjectives or, worse, turned up some inaccuracy. I grabbed my notes.

"No, no complaints from on high," said Philippe. "Not yet, at least. No, I've got a new assignment for you and it'll take you out of town." He leaned back and touched his fingers together, a smug gesture if he was smiling, a portentous one when he wasn't. He was smiling. "It's not anything big like the education exposé, just an interview this time, in the provinces. Could turn out to be nothing but it might prove interesting. Don't suppose you've ever heard of. . ." Philippe lowered his glasses from atop his bald head and picked up an index card. ". . . Mademoiselle Sophie Cordière?"

Still feeling relief, I said as agreeably as I could that I'd never heard of Sophie Cordière.

"A candidate for the National Assembly. Independent."

"What's the angle?"

"First naturalized refugee to do it-I mean, run for the Assembly."

"When did she become a citizen?"

He glanced at the card and answered dryly. "Two weeks ago last Tuesday."

"Really? A little premature to be running perhaps?"

"Or well calculated. Either way, it makes a story. Salimède, a school friend of mine, is retired and lives in the district. He insists she's some sort of Communist radical. He thinks she's dangerous."

"Dangerous?"

"Well, I suppose it's possible, but Salimède thinks half the people he meets are communists and all communists are dangerous."

"You really think there's a story in it?"

Philippe shrugged. "Worth a day-trip. Get you out of the city anyway. Oh, a couple more things. She officially changed her name the day before she filed her papers. Salimède is sure she's got a past."

"Everybody has a past."

"But most of us don't change our names. Do your research," warned Philippe officiously and handed over the index card. "Her real name's at the bottom. Salimède himself looked it up in the immigration records. I can't pronounce it. That should get you started. Au revoir, bon voyage, et bonne chance."

I checked. The name on Philippe's card was indeed the one on Mlle. Cordière's immigration record, her initial national identity card, and the document changing it to Sophie Cordière. But the unpronounceable name led to dead-ends. My wide search turned up records of over a dozen women who bore the same name. A few were deceased, others either too young or too old. Among those at about Mlle. Cordière's age, thirty-eight according to Philippe's index card, was a gynecologist living in Berne, an employee of an engineering firm in Dessau, and a professor of Slavic languages in British Columbia. There's also an interior designer in Buenos Aires, the proprietor of a furniture shop in Tunisia, a housewife in Bulgaria, and no less than two computer techs in Sweden.

I imagined a factory turning out mass-produced passports-same name, different photographs. My conclusion was that Sophie Cordière's real name was no more real than her new one and that France was most likely the end of a trail strewn with forged documents. This was quite likely a woman who'd been on the run, possibly someone in real danger. I wondered what she had done.

When I phoned to request an interview, Mlle. Cordière politely asked that I send my credentials by fax. I did so and got a prompt and positive reply suggesting we meet at her home in two days. "In the morning, around eleven, if that's convenient. If the conversation is congenial we could continue it over lunch." She gave me her address and directions from the railroad station.

I got up early to catch the first train, spent the first half of the trip dozing and the rest checking emails. The Education Ministry had released a response to my article that was both indignant and dissembling. Philippe was delighted.

Sophie Cordière's tiny second-floor apartment was in a shabby building on a charmless street in a rundown district half a mile from the town center. She was a good-looking woman, neither tall nor short, with pronounced cheekbones, sparkling brown eyes, dark eyebrows, unfashionably long hair, blonde to the roots. Her purple sweater and snug blue jeans showed her figure to advantage.

Her good looks were attractive rather than intimidating, quite unlike like those fashionable Parisiennes who like to weaponize their beauty. She greeted me at the door with a wry smile. To me, it displayed the irony of someone who isn't readily taken in by the world, who didn't take it or herself too seriously-or me, either.

The living room was barely large enough for a love-seat, one armchair, a small coffee table, and a bookcase with a portable television on top of it. The wallpaper was old and faded; the furniture looked second-hand.

She invited me to sit on the love-seat then offered both tea and coffee which I declined. When she was seated, I asked her permission to record the interview, though I'd also be taking notes on my laptop.

She sighed. "Who was it said that we live in an age that records everything and remembers nothing? Yes, of course. Sorry. Go ahead."

I took out my recorder and set it on the coffee table.

"Where do you want to begin?" she asked.

"With your name."

"Oh, my name. You know I changed it? Well, new job, new home, new name. I've had a number of them. My stage name was Gaia Gulova-less for the earth-mother than the alliteration."

"Why Sophie Cordière."

"Sophie's for wisdom, to which-like a seat in the National Assembly-I aspire. Cordière is a tribute to one of the great women of your country that has so generously taken me in, Louise Labé. You know Louise Labé?"

"I think I might have heard the name at school."

"Louise lived in the sixteenth century, a feminist avant le fait. Because she was the daughter of a rope-maker, she got the sobriquet of La Belle Cordière. In her youth, she excelled at horsemanship and archery and dressed as a man. She even armed herself as a man and fought as a knight at the Battle of Perpignan. It seems she even engaged in jousting. Imagine! A real amazon but not, apparently, a lesbian-at least to judge by her reputation. In Lyon, she started a literary salon and wrote, both prose and verse. Her poems were published along with twenty-four written in her honor, all by men who gushed. In general, I've found, the more sincere, the worse the poem."

This made me laugh. "Are they all so bad?"

She shrugged. "Some are better than others, of course. But Louise's sonnets are quite good, though restrained by the conventions of the times. The last of them begins Do not reproach me, Ladies, if I've loved / And felt a thousand torches burn my veins. It appears Madame Labé had a long string of lovers, pearls on a string, all glittering and cultured but none perfect. Calvin was scandalized by her cross-dressing. He called her a whore. I know what that's like."

I would naturally have liked to follow up on that last remark, but thought it better to get down to business. "Why are you running for office?"

"I came to this country, the country of Louise Labé, seeking refuge and found it. I was stateless and France has granted me citizenship. I want to pay back. I want to be an outstanding citizen. Besides, it's good for everyone to have both a hobby and an occupation, wouldn't you agree?"

"And which is politics for you, Mlle. Cordière? Hobby or occupation?"

She gave me a variation of the wry smile I'd seen at the door. "That will depend on the outcome of the election."

She stood up, went into what I presumed was her bedroom, and returned with an old scrapbook.

"For your amusement," she said, spreading it out beside me on the loveseat.

There were pictures cut from old newspapers with captions I couldn't decipher. She unfolded a splashy poster of dancers and three jazz musicians behind a singer with legs and arms akimbo.

She pointed. "Gaia Gulova, c'est moi!"

"You didn't overdress," I remarked.

"Still young enough not to need to. My prime was brief and in another country. Stale news now, but for a while men ran after me in herds-oh, and women too. Flowers and necklaces were the most popular inducements. Also, the most terrible poems-"

"The sincerest being the worst?"

"Precisely."

She held out her right hand and wiggled it.

"But I've always held on to this."

"Is that a ruby?"

"Yes. A real one, too."

"It's rather large."

"As vulgar as the man who gave it to me. That's why I won't part with it. He was a passionate and very tough union organizer. In those days, I was a proletarian pinup. Rubies are red and so was I-much redder than I am now, of course. These days I'm hardly even pink." She said this almost demurely and gave me yet another version of that smile I was already finding irresistible.

". . .Yes, back then I was bright scarlet. Well, conditions were bad. Bad food, bad air, bad police, bad government, bad everything. All the injustice made me angry and my indignation-I confess I wallowed in it-made me see more injustice. Tear everything down, that was my slogan back then. I used it as the refrain in one of the songs I wrote, a march and a good one, though it never caught on. I wasn't yet a politician. I wasn't a Saint Jeanne."

"What were you then?"

She touched a finger to her lips. "A post-adolescent vaudevillian with good legs."

"A vaudevillian?"

"It's an honorable profession, vaudeville-honorable though not respectable, like so many other fine things, just the opposite of so many dull professions."

"Such as?"

"Well, how about banking? 'What's robbing a bank compared to founding one?' That's Brecht, a good vaudevillian himself. Do you know where the word vaudeville comes from?"

"No."

"And yet you're French-more French than I am, you're thinking."

"We're both citizens, Mademoiselle."

"Oh yes, egalité, fraternité."

"Sororité too."

She scoffed. "If you say so."

"You'd describe yourself as a feminist?"

"What's that but a woman who thinks?"

"If you say so."

"Touché. Anyway, vaudeville. The word has a good working-class origin, right down to the mispronunciation. About a century before La Labé's heyday, a fuller named Basselin churned out lots of pop songs-drinking songs, love songs. War songs, too. He died fighting the English. Anyway, this Basselin was from the Val-de-Vire and might have been famous, but his songs were attributed to his birthplace rather than to the fuller. Val-de-Vire was slurred to vaudeville."

"Interesting. But what's a fuller?"

"Talk about working-class! Fullers cleaned and whitened wool. They had to pound and tread on it. The smelly job required ammonia. You can guess where that came from, I suppose. I expect Maître Basselin produced pissing songs too. I'd have enjoyed performing one of those for the comrades. They'd have loved it."

Mlle. Cordière said she'd like a cup of coffee and I said I'd join her. While she was in the kitchen, I examined her little library. It consisted of half-a-dozen books by left-wing political theorists; the rest were literary classics in various languages including a volume of Louise Labé's works. I took that one out. I skimmed the love sonnets, direct and intensely passionate-too good to be sincere? There was also a prose dialogue titled The Debate Between Love and Folly. Perhaps the woman felt these were the poles of her life; maybe Sophie Cordière did too.

The coffee was delicious.

We resumed.

"Question?"

"How would you describe your political views?"

"Ah, getting to the point at last. Well, my opponents from all sides are calling me a radical. Fair enough, but not accurate. Radix. Latin for root. I suppose a radical is what I was once, since I wanted to tear weeds up by the root. But, as mentioned, I've moderated my views. I'm no longer so hot-blooded or optimistic. When I hear people touting utopian dreams and colossal social engineering projects, I feel like saying something sarcastic. I don't agree with technology-besotted youngsters who imagine a sleek, smooth world into which they would deposit equally sleek, smooth citizens. Free markets are really good at generating wealth, but when have they ever been free or fair in distributing the loot? The prospect of changing people's insides by amending the outside excited me when I was young. To change is to ought was a challenge that energized me. So much was wrong! The country in which I found myself was one big scandal. Not surprising then that I was moved to join young people like myself who wanted to blow it all up and build something better on the ruins. At that age and in that place, I'd have been ashamed not to have joined. But now I think we must begin more humbly and modestly, with something more reliable and less nebulous than dreams."

"And what is that? What's the more reliable platform?"

"We must begin with human nature, the rock on which utopias always founder. Human nature is one of the great conservative forces, like money, inertia, and language. I've learned to respect human nature and also Newton's First Law."

"It's surprising to hear you praise conservatism."

"Not conservatism and not praise, just respect. Different things."

"Point taken. But can you tell me-and my readers-a bit more about what you mean by human nature?"

"Oui, bien sûr. I take it as the first axiom that people are born self-interested. Who's more selfish than an infant? The second axiom is that most people gradually become aware, with more or less clarity, that they belong to a social species. I conclude that by nature we're squeezed between freedom and necessity, isolated bags of skin nonetheless bound to others. Politics, as I see it, ought to acknowledge the first axiom and remind people of the second. I favor policies that don't coerce-much less crush-the individual and her liberty but increase the coherence and, above all, the decency of society."

"I'm not sure I follow. Could you give an example? A policy?"

"Certainly. Our first priority must be to save the planet from becoming as uninhabitable as its neighbors. We have the freedom to burn hydrocarbons, raze rainforests, and crosshatch the sky with contrails. Freedom to do such things is exercised not just by profiteering corporations abetted by short-sighted governments but also by indifferent individuals-which is to say voters. This has put us and our descendants in peril along with the innocent flora and fauna. People keep their eyes down and argue over pensions and potholes, ignoring the looming tsunami rushing toward us."

"So, you're a Green? An Eco-Warrior?"

She made a wiping gesture. "Stow the labels, please. I'm an independent in solidarity with my fellow creatures, a solitary member of the collective."

"If you say so. But, back to your platform."

"Yes. So far, the political response to the obvious crisis has been laughably inadequate. What's almost worse is that everybody knows it. Democratic politics are like God-both give us free will which means we can choose the bad as readily as the good."

"Excuse me. You believe in God?"

"Again, you've mistaken me-not on purpose, I hope. But, since you ask, I'd say that at least six days out of the week, I'm an atheist."

"And on the other? You rest?"

"Ah, a wit! Let's say it varies. I believe that faith without doubt is stupidity."

"And what of doubt without faith?"

"Unsustainable. We can't prove we've got free will any more than we can prove there's a God-or that a decent economy provides the greatest good for the greatest number. In that respect, all faiths resemble each other. Either you assent or you don't. But suppose for a moment that there is a God and this God has granted us free will. What would he want us to do with it? To be entertaining or to freely choose what's good? For either alternative, we don't require God since he made us free even of him. God's like my old audiences, an onlooker. Look, all I'm saying is that good politicians should respect everybody's freedom but give encouragement to choose the better, wiser path. The trick is to enact the good without forcing it down people's throats. Do that and the good ceases to be good."

"Is this why you've proposed extending our system of public transportation and making it free?"

"The people will be free but, of course, transportation isn't."

"Thus, your proposed your new system of taxation?"

"Absolutely. Fifty percent of all corporate profits, all private, unearned incomes, and all salaries over a fixed minimum to be dedicated to restructuring transport, agricultural and energy sectors before it's too late. I don't see any other alternative. The decisions, however, of corporate managers and individual consumers will be left entirely to them."

"Excuse me, but won't these new taxes, which your opponents call-with some reason-'confiscatory,' divorce economic freedom from personal and political freedom?"

She sighed. "Listen. If you give a child ten dollars to buy toys, she's just as free to choose her purchases as if you gave her fifty. In the country where I was born, the peasants had a saying: Even a pauper can choose to sleep on his back or his side. Now, I'm famished. What do you say we grab some lunch? There's a workers' bistro two blocks away. It's clean and the food's not bad."

As we walked, she waved and accosted those who didn't smile back, informing them she was running to represent them in the National Assembly. She introduced me as a reporter from the capital where her candidacy had generated great interest, then she asked everyone what they'd like her to do if she won. Few of the women said anything, but all the men answered, some at length. The reply that seemed to please her best was from an old pensioner who shuffled along with a cane. "Do what the liar in office promised to do and didn't: take from the rich and give to the poor."

"Yes," said the candidate taking his hand. "That would make a change."

The bistro was modest and not crowded. They already knew her there, greeting her by her new name. She asked for a salade niçoise. On her recommendation, I ordered the onion soup. We shared a bottle of vin ordinaire.

I took out my recorder. "Can we talk about your past?"

"Off the record or on?"

"On-but off if you insist. Does it matter?"

She shrugged and gave her hair a toss. "Not really."

Sophie Cordière spoke freely about herself, though I've no idea how truthfully.

"It was during one of my native country's interludes between dictatorships that I became a semi-celebrity. I went on tour and drew good notices everywhere. I sang, I danced, I told funny stories. Sometimes I recited my own poetry, but I always wound things up with a speech-a fiery one."

"What were your speeches about?"

"Important things like freedom and humanity and justice. Big ideas, big feelings. But my speeches didn't work the way I wanted. I used to blame the audiences, only wanting to be entertained and not roused. Now I understand that my harangues were too abstract."

"I know what you mean. I've sat through more than a few excruciatingly tedious rousing speeches."

"Really? Well, maybe mine were tedious. But I enjoyed giving them. When I denounced injustice, I felt more righteous; when I praised freedom, I felt freer."

"Do you think if you'd enjoyed speaking a little less, your speeches might have gone over better?"

"A shrewd point. You may be right. Only the police-and I'm proud to say the police were always at my performances-only the police took any notice of what I said. What interested everybody else was how I looked, how vivacious, sexy, and flamboyant. Even if they didn't care what I said, they could tell what I was just by looking. Sometimes I couldn't bear their stares-the ogling men, the judging women worse-and then I'd wind up the performance with a sardonic Charleston and a rude gesture. Our little company lived together in a big old apartment in the capital. We were squatters and crusaders, creative collaborators, bohemians. It was a wonderful time, really. We were devoted to our mission. We performed right up to the end."

She paused then repeated sadly, "The end. When they came for us."

I waited for her to go on. "There's nothing you'd like to add?"

"I'd simply like you to understand. There wasn't any middle ground to dance on. Only lucky countries can afford moderation."

"Does a lucky country mean a rich one, or do you believe it's one that's built solid institutions and sticks by them?"

She thought about that for a moment. "Not mutually exclusive, are they? But I don't know." She shrugged. "The people where I come from excel at drunken joy but have no talent for happiness."

"You equate happiness with moderation? That's surprising for someone called a radical."

"Ex-radical," she said sharply. "We've covered that."

"Do you believe this country has a talent for happiness?"

"Why, it's famous for it! Oh yes, France has a talent for happiness as much as for protesting and striking. In fact, all the protesting and striking are the result of expecting to be happy, as if happiness were the natural condition of things. On the happiness chart, I believe France comes in third, behind Denmark and Bhutan. My aim's to make my new country still happier and move it up the list."

Remarkable, how smoothly she transitioned into campaign mode, her voice louder, her expression more ingratiating.

"I'd like to go back to the past again, if that's all right."

"Yes?"

"How old were you when you left your country?"

"I was twenty-four. And I barely made it out. Most of my friends didn't."

This is what I was after, not policies but a story.

"What happened?"

"The respite between dictatorships came to a sudden end, like all the others. The police bided their time and went on filing their reports. Tommy, my manager, was the first to be arrested. They dragged him right out of the Café Magus at three in the afternoon. That was because they wanted the news to spread fast. At three o'clock, the Magus was always filled with our sort. Maybe not being first on their list was what my celebrity bought me. More likely they figured Tommy, the oldest among us, was our ringleader. Poor Tommy. He cared a lot about his dignity. He even had business cards! How humiliated he must have been-dragged away in front of the comrades. It must have been almost as bad as being tortured. I still have bad dreams about Tommy."

"Such as?"

"In one, he's horribly emaciated, in rags and chained to the floor of a medieval dungeon. He sits there bravely reciting Brecht poems to an audience of rats."

"Reciting poems? Any particular poem?"

"I remember the one called Seven Hundred Intellectuals Pray to an Oil Tanker."

"Are you suggesting they took your manager first to warn you? Was somebody was trying to protect you?"

"For a while I wondered about that. Not now. Within two hours, they'd arrested Georg, Herman, and Andrej. I'm sure they meant to round us all up at once and just missed me and Bella and Milena, my backup singers. Bella and Milena were sisters and good friends to me. Jaffar, our pianist, took off on his motorcycle as soon as he heard about Tommy. I learned later that he made it to the frontier. Seems he tried to disguise himself as a Muslim lady-a Muslim lady on a motorcycle. Poor Jaffar! He was so meticulous about his cross-dressing, so elegant, and he was caught in a plaid flannel skirt and a phony hijab. Maybe he'd have had a better chance if he could have laid his hands on a niqab."

"What happened to Tommy and Jaffar and the others?"

"What do you think?"

"I see. And how about your escape?"

"Oh, my escape was dramatic but also rather funny. Milena said she'd take her parents' car. The three of us dressed up as men and put on long overcoats. We all had ski balaclavas. The girls phoned their cousin Gustave. He bought us toy pistols. The plan was to pass ourselves off as a special police squad rushing to round people up. The irony appealed to us, but it was ludicrous, of course. We laughed about it ourselves. We parked the car in an alley, ate cold goulash out of a can, and waited until midnight. Then we took off for the border."

"You thought the border guards would let you cross?"

"I know! It was crazy. I was to tell them in my deepest deep voice that we'd been sent to apprehend a pair of high-value targets who'd made it across the night before. I'd say we knew their whereabouts and were under orders to track them down and liquidate them."

"And that worked?"

"Of course not. There were two guards, both sleepy, but one was suspicious. What did the trick was the toy guns. When they asked for our papers, Milena and I aimed the plastic pistols at them. Bella gave a whoop, floored the accelerator, and we blew straight through the barrier."

"It's quite a story."

"As I said, it was dramatic but also laughable."

"Why did the new regime want to arrest your whole circle?"

"The whole troupe, you should say. Why go after inoffensive vaudevillians? Is that what you mean? I'd say it was for or the same reason Calvin called Louise a whore. We offended them. Our views were exactly the ones they feared. We were young and they were old. We didn't live by family values. We read the wrong books and sang the wrong tunes. Our popularity was a threat, too. If we continued to speak out, people might listen. Some of them, anyway. As for me, they hated how I looked, the way I dressed-the titillation perhaps even more than the politics. Actually, I doubt they saw much of a distinction between the two."

"You like being provocative?"

"I did back then. Well, maybe I still do. Politically, that is."

She smiled at me. She knew that I was flirting.

It was a fine afternoon. After we left the bistro, I suggested we walk for a while then go back to her apartment.

"I beg your pardon, but I thought the interview was over. There's something else you want to ask me?"

"Well. . . one thing."

"Yes?"

"Is there a man in your life? Readers will be interested."

"No. Not a single man."

"A woman?"

"Likewise, no."

I knew I was about to be dismissed.

She made a show of checking her watch. "Look, I have to speak to a group of sanitation workers in two hours. I need to prepare."

"Two hours? But that's plenty of time."

And it was.

I wrote the beginning of my article that night:

Sophie Cordière is the first refugee to aspire to the National Assembly. Her political career is more likely to be short than long. She belongs to no party, but she is a remarkable person who could win against the odds. If she succeeds, she will introduce an original alto voice to the Assembly's monotonous chorus. Mlle. Cordière is a woman of the Left but with original views. Though she is most likely to figure as the smallest of political footnotes, she is a charismatic speaker fully capable of outclassing our pedestrian party leaders. In any event, her aims are in accord with her chosen name. Rope is made by braiding what is the thin and weak into something strong and resilient.

After typing this, I phoned Philippe and asked if he could spare me for another couple of days.

"It's a good story," I said lamely, "but complicated."

Philippe just laughed.

I visited Sophie again, just before the election, which she won narrowly. I couldn't get away, so we celebrated by phone and email.

Sophie was sworn in, took her seat, made her maiden speech. It was modest, rather than rousing; sensible, yet urgent. Now that she was in Paris, I saw her as often as she would allow.

Then, as everyone knows, she was brutally attacked on the steps of the Assembly, like Caesar. Stabbed ten times.

The assassin was a young man, initially thought to be a right-wing fanatic. He turned out to be a spurned lover.

"Not a single man," she'd said. Misleading, but technically accurate.

I've been reading Louise Labé's love sonnets, especially the one Sophie quoted to me. I'll give the final word to La Belle Cordière.

Ladies, do not denigrate my name.

If I did wrong, the pain and punishment

Are now. Don't file their daggers to a point.

You must know, Love is master of the game.

THE POETS' STRIKE

Afterwards, the editors of the better periodicals claimed to have noticed a decline in the quality of submissions, though no corresponding decrease in quantity. "We published the best of the worst," they admitted. Black-clad, baseball-capped, samite-gowned, scatologically explicit performers went on declaiming at the usual slams. The immortal dead continued to be dissected in desiccated classrooms all over the planet, repelling most, inspiring few. Even as corpses, the masters went on chanting their non-biodegradable verses. Contests were still announced, awards duly distributed. In short, the deprivation was invisible.

Only later, when the existence of the strike became widely known, was it possible to account for certain previously inexplicable events. For example, on Bastille Day sunbathers on the Côte D'Azur were alarmed when two biplanes painted in primary colors banked low over the beach at Nice then flew on, scattering blank sheets of paper all the way to Cannes. At the inauguration of the ultra-nationalistic President of Slovakia, the new laureate, before being dragged from the dais, mumbled under his breath half a page from a Mozambican telephone directory. A few baffling incidents could now be interpreted as a sort of picketing, though the locations appeared random and the messages blurred, as though aimed more at preventing a design from being discerned rather than bringing the world to its knees. In September, three middle-aged women dressed in olive-drab jumpsuits marched for two hours outside a delicatessen in Paterson, New Jersey carrying signs that read "Hats off! Beneath the sidewalk, the beach!" A week later six young men in white head cloths assumed the lotus position and chanted "Cavilcante" beside the entrance to a driving range in Kasukabe, Japan. Early in November, a dark, elderly man-it was the great Balinese poet Halachim Ligana, a registered national treasure in Indonesia-stood stoic and silent for eight hours outside the gates of an oil refinery in

Cabimas, Venezuela. The workers laughed at him on the way to and from their shifts. I might list a dozen similar incidents. Who could figure them out or even connect them? These pickets, if that is what they were, never set up outside the offices of literary agents or publishing houses, never blocked the marble vestibules or clogged the opulent lobbies of Arts Councils, Foundations, Ministries of Culture.

So, in its first phase, the strike was, so to speak, a cryptic conceit, a complaint without a whine. It seems that, as originally conceived, the strike was to be an absurd trope, intended more as a snub or prank than a warning. There was no hint of anguish in it. Perhaps later, when the strike spread like a virus from one nation to another, or, more precisely, from one distinguished poet to the next, it was transformed. It lost its antic quality as a sort of happening or piece of conceptual art and turned more sober. The strike might have persisted for its own sake, with its own momentum and implications. Silence always implies protest, and the most unsettling of protests is the one lacking an identifiable object.

Looking back, people like to imagine that the strike did not go entirely unnoticed, that we felt vague wishes to hear the weather described better than the TV meteorologists could manage, some apprehension that the world suddenly lacked a dimension on which, though crucial, one couldn't quite put one's finger. The truth is less flattering. Even as the press was converting the stunt into a worldwide story there were plenty to say, "What a laugh! We've got more than enough of the old stuff to hold out indefinitely. And who wants even the old stuff, let alone the new?"

But there was no dearth of the new. After all, not everyone who oozes verse is a poet. Indeed, once the strike became public knowledge, this distinction became so clear that to elucidate it might almost have been the purpose of the strike itself. Once the story caught the imagination of the public, people realized that anybody still composing verses must ipso facto be a charlatan, or worse-a scab.

The existence of strikebreakers, dismissed in news reports as a false rumor, was real. What I have thus far recorded is generally known, but to understand these scabs it is necessary to tell another story, the one at the core of the strike, its true history.

One day last April, Jorge Luchetti walked into the Buenos Aires headquarters of the Papyrus Corporation, a powerful though little-known multinational holding company. He left a message for the chairman announcing a poets' strike, which he claimed to have instigated. This Luchetti, a slim thirty-year-old with large eyes and unruly hair, taught occasional university classes in English and French literature though he did not hold a regular appointment. Most of his income came from small translating and editing jobs for local publishers. His background, however, was distinguished. The Luchettis are a prominent Argentine family. Jorge's mother is on the board of several charitable institutions, including an orphanage. Jorge's father owns a string of popular bakeries spread over the length of the country and for some years he was active in liberal politics. Jorge's older brother is a provincial commissioner of police, his one sister a successful painter of landscapes. Jorge was the Luchetti family's black sheep.

Jorge's thirty-six published poems never attracted much attention. Though my Spanish is not at all bad I am far from an expert in the intricacies of that language's verse. From what I have seen, his poems appear to be adroit and well crafted, but conventional and uninspired. A few of the shorter lyrics are arresting, though. Luchetti did have talent, but this talent lay in negativity, which is to say not in writing poems about death so much as in arranging the death of poems. As a negotiator, he proved much the same: gifted, morose, unforthcoming, and unresponsive. I am an executive of the Papyrus Corporation, and I was assigned the task of meeting with Luchetti. It was as a negotiator, not a poet, that I came to know him.

"What is it you want?" I asked him bluntly at our first meeting.

He only glanced at me impassively and fingered his white linen trousers.

I adopted a derisive tone. "Respect? Subsidies? To be better understood? Sympathy for your tender sensitivities?"

He looked up with a sad little smile. "Go on," he said. His voice was surprisingly high-pitched. He sounded like a tenor but looked like a baritone.

"What then? A new anthology? More prizes? Purification of tongues? An International Poets' Day?"

He made round motions with his pale hand.

"TV programs devoted to the reading of sonnets? Standardization of forms? Regular salaries from the state?"

He shrugged. "When the demands are met, you'll know."

"Demands? But that's what I'm asking you about. What demands?"

He grinned. "That's for you to find out."

Of course, these negotiations did not begin at once. Luchetti was thrown out of my company's offices on that April day, dismissed as a madman. And yet what he claimed was true. That is, Jorge Luchetti had indeed initiated a poets' strike. To do it he used the computer at the office of one of the publishers that employed him as a translator. His showing up there at odd hours would not have surprised anyone. Astonishingly, the whole affair was set in motion by just a few score e-mail messages. Luchetti had struck a chord with his colleagues.

It was the bleak poet Jean-Philippe Drouillard, member of the French Academy, who first broke the story to a reporter at Le Figaro. I doubt that this was part of Luchetti's plan, but what French intellectual could resist introducing any novel cultural development into la discours? The story was quickly confirmed with nods from two Nobel Prize winners, one Polish, the other Nigerian. In no more than a day, the story was picked up everywhere. Hundreds of news programs across the planet chose it as the jolly bit with which to wind up their evening broadcasts on December 7.

Luchetti had shown shrewdness in approaching a multinational corporation rather than, say, one of the better-known literary critics. The latter would certainly have misunderstood him, but businessmen grasped, if not the meaning of the strike, then the precedent it represented. In an age of globalization, any successful international labor action is of the highest significance. To corporations like mine the strike was not a joke but a threat.

Now for the scabs. The multinationals, communicating back and forth with the alacrity that characterizes our epoch, quickly agreed on three strategies, running from soft to hard. I was chosen to negotiate with Luchetti who, as the originator of the strike, was deemed the best candidate to end it. Negotiation was the softest alternative. The second tactic, better fitted to commodity and raw materials boycotts, was to flood the market. Executives and secretaries, particularly, though not exclusively, those with undergraduate degrees in the liberal arts, were re-assigned to produce a set quota of poems each day. Chapbooks and anthologies rolled daily off presses throughout the world. But then the story got out. People realized that, as all the real poets were striking-and how many authentic poets are there in any generation?-anybody still being published could not be the genuine article. Reviews of all new work seethed with ridicule.

There was an unanticipated consequence of this second tactic. Here and there in corner offices and exiguous cubicles some of those put to the task of writing bad poems found that they could write good ones. This must have caused them some perplexity, dividing loyalties, mixing motives, and challenging self-concepts. These people began to hide their poems, refusing to turn them over to the bosses, in effect joining the strikers. Others went still further and quit their jobs. To understand these people one must recall the prestige of being a poet at that time. At no period in modern history has there been more glamour, more sex appeal in being a poet than during the strike; yet this and the allure of dignity could be attained solely by an unwillingness to produce decent poems. Restraint. Silence. Gagging the Muse and locking her away in a closet. The strike may not have raised the demand for poetry, but there is no doubt that it increased the supply of poets. The corporations soon found that they were losing numbers of their most promising middle managers. The consequent pressure fell on me.

Much to my surprise, at our last meeting Luchetti handed me a poem. Perhaps he had grown fond of me or, more likely, he elected this method of mocking my efforts, intending to show me where they would wind up. Anyway, it was his final poem. It includes the following lines of which I offer this free translation:

. . . the twin cadenzas of her orchestral

legs; the innocent grace notes behind each

breathtaking knee. Death shall be a lutelike

pavanne, sweetly strummed by swanlike hands.

From these overwrought, prophetic verses, typical of Luchetti's rococo style, I conclude that he anticipated our third tactic. True enough, all his poems are as full of death as the cup my secretary just brought me is of coffee. Heaven knows why his death should trouble me. A young man unable to cope with life, at odds with his family and the world, flamboyantly depressive, half in love with easeful death-what was he but a candidate for suicide? And yet Luchetti's demise, which brought an end to the strike, was not a suicide, at least not in the usual sense. Moreover, a poet's work need not be read literally. I remind myself that an obsession with the theme of death hardly obligates a writer to kill himself. In the case of a man like Luchetti, still young enough to feel himself immortal, still confident of his own potential, there may have been nothing more to his morose verses than a Romantic pose. In fact, one might justly say that his poems are as crammed with life as death, with all the sensations, pleasures, and irritations of existence.

After the failure of my negotiations, I was not informed of anything; nevertheless, I have used my connections to discover that the person sent to do the job sent was a woman.

HORATIA

What to wear? I had gone to bed to escape the question, and more serious ones, too. When I woke-early, nervous, excited-I had to smile. Worrying about my clothes? Apart from my street-bought J'Aime Paris sweatshirt and old gray sweatpants I had only two options, the purple dress and the black, neither what a Parisienne would call chic. Black had too many undesirable connotations, so the purple it would have to be, a slightly faded but respectable frock, plain, unflattering, with nothing imperial about it. If I'd had more time before fleeing, I might have taken more clothes. If I'd had more money, I might have gone shopping the previous afternoon, maybe picking out a serious Clinton-Merkel pantsuit. A sequined jumper would have been eye-catching. Or, still better, a cool, provocatively form-fitting leather jacket. Well, I lacked both the time and the money, so it was just a case of imaginary lèche-vitrine, another way to distract myself from the day's ordeal. Even my vanity was another diversion because I knew the purple or the black were fit enough for the likes of me. I wasn't auditioning for stardom; yet in a few hours I was likely to be seen by thousands of people. It requires a lot of modesty and humility to be equal to that prospect. My feelings were the same I had before my first recital. What was I then? Seven or eight? Did this emotional regression cheapen my current feeling or lend more solemnity to my childish ones? More thoughts to distract myself. Dread of humiliation, exposure, fear of failure-don't these carry the same weight at any age, like hate and love?

It was just my second day in Paris. I enjoyed speaking school French. I thought of the Racine we had to read and the Baudelaire that was forbidden. The day before, on the street, I heard a vendor speaking Italian and a couple speaking Spanish. The Romance languages all have their own music, as do the countries that speak them. Vivaldi's nothing like de Falla, and you'd never mistake Debussy for Respighi. Yet all these languages were once Latin and all these countries part of an Empire Europeans have never gotten out of their system. Spanish, Italian, French-what a triumph for mispronunciation! Sumru and I took French and English together, likewise literature, math, and history-everything except the courses about which we cared the most- political economy for Sumru, music for me. We sometimes spoke French to one another, pretending we were in Paris ordering elaborate banquets or in Cannes raving about Truffaut. How I wished she were with me, though it was just because she wasn't in Paris that I was.

Sumru Erkat's name is known to many and I'm about to try to make it known to many more. My name is Veta Demirkan. I am now an ex-public-school music teacher and quondam mediocre performer on the violin and viola. There is no reason you should take the slightest interest in me. The list of things that I'm not-beautiful, smart, rich, talented, strong-is dwarfed by the catalogue of what I am-ordinary, craven, plain, less than clever. And yet I am a significant character in the story I'm attempting to tell, though not the protagonist or heroine. That's Sumru. She is and always has been a princess, a glass of fashion, a star from a prominent family, noble and outspoken-"Who by?" I once joked, admiringly. Sumru is all that I am not.

The Erkat family are among the aristocrats of the city. They had wealth, an old name, a reputation for philanthropy and probity. The Erkats have furnished the republic with some of its most distinguished public officials, including the brave public prosecutor whose assassination led to the fall of a government and whose death is still commemorated annually, or was until this year.

At school, Sumru was also a star. I was from an obscure family, more diligent than talented at my schoolwork. It was a mystery why Sumru should have plucked me from the subterranean social stratum reserved for scholarship girls at Lady Mihri Academy to make me her best friend. I couldn't possibly ask at the time but, years later, I did. I'm still not sure how seriously to take her answer. "Oh, that? It was simply because I saw at once how unlike me you are," said Sumru.

"You mean not pretty or rich?"

Sumru scoffed. "Don't be absurd. No, I mean you stay off emotional rollercoasters. I admired that. You've always been so sane and-oh, what's the word?-equable. You're logical and I liked that because my own logic so often breaks down."

Equable and logical I may have been. Perhaps that's why I was drawn to music and mathematics and not Sumru's penchant for political causes. But I was grateful. Maybe she sensed that she would find in me not just an anti-self but also a faithful, if tongue-tied, loyalist.

The first words Sumru spoke to me were an invitation. After history class one day, she left the group of girls that was always gathered around her, strode right up to me and said, "Can you get permission to come home with me after school on Thursday?" The Can you was superfluous, but I was grateful for Sumru's courtesy, her respect for my dignity.

Our school, the best girls' school in the city, was named for Mihri Hatun, called the "Sappho of the Ottomans," who died in 1506. It's not surprising that I would come to identify my friend with Lady Mihri. In my mind, they were the same type. True, Mihri grew up to write poetry and Sumru editorials; but though their subjects and genres were different, their passion and beauty were the same. I remember entertaining the fantasy that Mihri was reborn in my friend. Mihri Hatun was the daughter of a judge, "beautiful and ardent" the official biography declares -but never married. We are given to understand that she "fell in love many times but all these loves were chaste." Mihri's poems certainly confirm the first part, anyway:

> At one glance
> I love you
> With a thousand hearts. . .

> My body, whirling, is a lighthouse
> Illuminated by your image.
>
> Let zealots think
> Loving is sinful
> Never mind
> Let me burn in the hellfire
> Of that sin.

Sumru too was quick to fall in love and relished burning, though I'm sure she never thought the fire infernal or love sinful. Her adolescent infatuations were like so many jabs, sharp and short. She would fixate on a boy glimpsed on the street, a new teacher, David Beckham, the nephew of one of her father's business associates, Johnny Depp-even, for a few weeks, Lord Byron. She could be just as passionate about football, movies, and deceased social theorists. Her father, though a merchant rather than a judge, could certainly be judgmental. Mr. Erkat was unsettled by his daughter's blazing enthusiasms and anxious about her virginity. He might have saved himself the worry; for Sumru was as unlikely to engage physically with the boy on the street or the new teacher as with Ludwig Feuerbach or Lord Byron. What was true in her wasn't the feeling fixed on an ostensible object but the feeling itself. Her ardent nature would later find another, more consequential, outlet, and in this she too was as chaste as Mihri. You could even say that Sumru's passion is what led to my being in a room rented for me by a Parisian press organization, steeling myself to face cameras and speak into microphones.

After we graduated, I went to the Teachers College to study music. Sumru enrolled in university and, to please her father, chose to concentrate in business, though she took all the political science courses she could. During those years, we saw each other as often as we could, still the faithful dyad we had been since girlhood.

Sumru and I often spoke of our families, especially our fathers. They were of distinct classes, with different origins, yet they resembled each other. Both were conservative, pious, content with the status-quo, proud of us and determined to see that we would have a good future. The unusual thing was that they wanted to see us educated just as much as they wanted us married.

"My father says I should go off to London or Frankfurt after the degree. In a general way, he even has my husband picked out. He'll be some boy from a good family doing the same thing."

"Would you like to?"

"Marry an expat capitalist? Not particularly."

"I mean go to Europe."

"Oh, Europe's like a museum. Half the people there don't want people like us even to visit."

"So, you don't want to go then?"

"To get called names? To get fixed up in Germany or the UK with somebody's precious first-born boy?"

"Well, if you don't want to go abroad, what would you like to do?"

"I wish I knew, Veta. I want to do something I can throw myself into, that'll make me hate to get into bed at night and leap out of it every morning." She laughed at herself then grinned at me-no need for her to say that her best friend wouldn't want such a frantic life, that I preferred to keep my emotional chart flat.

Sumru talked brilliantly about the authors she read both in and out of class, writers about whom I knew only what she told me. She favored disturbers of the peace, difficult, abstract thinkers with outlandish names like Antonio Gramsci, Luce Iragary, Max Horkheimer. She favored radicals, the flaming kind who wrote long, complex sentences. It was the way it was with her old crushes; she embraced trends but didn't stick with them long. I would try to keep up by talking about my own enthusiasms but did it clumsily. I can play music, but find it hard to talk about it. I worked at it, though, preparing things to say like, "If differential equations could sing and dance, they'd sound like Bach." Lame.

I remember her saying once as we sat in our favorite café, "I wish I could hear music the way you do. I mean serious music. Your music."

It was as if she had made me the proprietor of Debussy, Chopin, and Mahler.

"Why don't you?"

"Oh, why," she said with the impatient toss of her head I knew so well. "Don't know, really. I suppose it's the way it makes me feel."

"How?"

"Caged. Big cages, gorgeous ones, but still cages. And manipulated. When I try listening to serious music, it's overwhelming. It's as if the music's saying things I can't grasp but forcing me to swallow them. Wagner, for instance. A total totalitarian. Pop tunes don't mean much, but they set me free. I mean, you can't really dance to that what's-his-name, Bruckner, can you?"

Sumru graduated a week before I did. She came to my ceremony and took me to lunch two days later. She was exhilarated.

"I've reached a decision. I'm going to get my father to turn over that second-rate newspaper he owns to me. The Salah Gazete. You know it?"

"No, not really."

"I'm not surprised. The rag's so dull and dusty that nobody reads it. It's failing. But I've got some ideas."

"Will he give it to you?"

Sumru smiled and looked fifteen again. "Before it folds? Maybe. If I can keep from being sent into exile and nag him enough."

The nagging took three months.

Sumru did have ideas for the Gazete. She added cartoons and flashy fashion pieces with color photographs. She recruited two decent columnists, one a feisty and funny middle-aged feminist, the other one of her classmates who-with self-mockery-called himself an anarchist and tried to dress the part. Sumru produced lively editorials too, liberal rather than radical. Sales of the Gazete picked up. Mr. Erkat mentioned Frankfurt and London less often but continued to harp on marriage, as did my father. Our mothers were less insistent on the matter. It wasn't that either disagreed, just that they were content to leave the pestering to our fathers.

In my first year teaching music in a primary school, I got a serious boyfriend, a colleague. He'd looked at me too long when we passed in the corridors and constantly during faculty meetings. Ihsan taught history but his real love was classical poetry. He knew all about Lady Mihri. Whenever I performed with some amateur trio or quartet he always came and, at the end, jumped to his feet and applauded louder than anybody else. It didn't matter how awful we were.

With a good deal of trepidation, I introduced Ihsan and Sumru. They didn't hit it off. Neither would say anything bad about the other to me, but I could see from their body language that they were inimical. They leaned away from one another. I considered that Sumru was too critical, mercurial, too intellectual, and altogether too contemporary for Ihsan. For his part, I supposed Ihsan might appear too complacent and too devoted to the past for Sumru. To her, history was just dead politics and classical poetry antiquated. We didn't get together more than a few times and I can't recall either ever asking after the other.

Then came the changes. A new government came to power and the new president called a vote to change the constitution in ways that would augment the powers of his office to be followed by a general election aimed at putting more of his supporters in parliament. To all this the military acceded. The conservatives in the countryside liked the president because he never had a good word for the city or its young people. They also approved of his sanctimoniously invoking the Deity before and after every speech. The new constitution was narrowly approved. A few demonstrations were organized and one of them got out of hand. There were arrests. Sumru wrote a caustic editorial that provoked her father to remind her that he was also her publisher.

During this time, we met at our usual café. "My darling baba believes he can accommodate himself to any government because any government will have to accommodate itself to people like him." Sumru put her wrath into her hands, making fists on the iron café table, but her face suggested that she was perfectly happy.

I did something rare for me. I ventured a joke. "You look like an indignant saint."

"An indignant saint? Well, you're half right anyway."

Then came the general election campaign and the country split like a ripe pomegranate. You'd be hard pressed to find anybody who hadn't taken a side. Even conversations that began over the price of peppers, praise of a new grandchild, the dry weather, ended in politics. At one faculty meeting, as everybody around me argued and fretted, I proposed that for every minute spent watching the news, we should all devote two to looking at trees.

The liberal parties unified behind one candidate under the banner of popular government, human rights, and personal freedom. The president's party preached fear and piety. The campaign was bitter and sometimes violent. A few people were killed. People from both sides were arrested, but those of the president's party were immediately released.

Of course, The Sabah Gazete stood firmly against the president. Sumru's editorials, never less than forceful but patiently argued, grew less restrained, then downright strident. Her columnists barked more loudly; the cartoonists bit more deeply. She showed up regularly at rallies and, on two occasions, took the microphone herself to speak on the rights of women. There were rows with her father. "He wants me to keep my head below the parapet. His exact words. As if this were the First World War." While she wouldn't give in to his pleas, she wasn't angry with him because she understood that her baba was also torn. He was reluctant to close down the Gazete for fear of alienating his daughter, but also because he didn't believe she was wrong. Mr. Erkat no longer felt so confident about those smooth accommodations between business and politics. Like many other men of affairs, he grew anxious about the direction of events. I suppose he moved money out of the country a little at a time.

Sumru phoned me just after the results of the vote were announced by the Electoral Commission.

"Can you believe it? 84%! What a joke."

"No, it doesn't sound right," I said weakly.

"Everybody knew the Commission was crooked. The foreign observers don't believe it. And they've said so."

"Will that matter?"

"It ought to."

Listening to her tone, that of an indignant saint, I began to worry about Sumru. "What are you going to do?"

"Pick up a copy of today's paper, Veta."

A week later, one of my erudite colleagues explained that the headline Sumru stuck atop her front-page editorial was a play on a maxim of La Rochefoucauld, converting the Frenchman's cynicism into her idealism. In bold face, the Gazete proclaimed Rigged Elections are The Tribute Paid by Despotism to Democracy.

After that, events moved with shattering swiftness. Clearly, the government had laid their plans. All the liberal journals and three radio stations were closed down on the same day, and the only independent television channel taken over by the state. Sumru's father was compelled to sell the Gazete to a friend of the president for a ridiculously low price. In my one telephone conversation with Mr. Erkat, he told me why he had agreed. The leverage was his daughter's freedom-but that was a lie. Sumru disappeared the day after the sale agreeent signed. The police claimed they had no idea where she was. "Perhaps she's gone to London-or to Frankfurt," an intelligence officer suggested to the desperate Mr. Erkat, with a knowing smirk.

I wrote a petition, found a place to run off a thousand copies, and circulated them to everybody I could think of. I gave copies to colleagues, neighbors, cousins, even some of my older students. The opposition called for a protest demonstration, and I was asked to be one of the speakers, an utterly terrifying prospect. But I did it. I brought along copies of my petition calling for Sumru's immediate release and read it aloud. Hundreds signed before the police broke things up.

That afternoon Ihsan showed up at my door. He looked stricken and also a little sheepish, a man doing what he felt obliged to do but not wanting to do it. I didn't have to wait to find out how things stood.

His first words were a rhetorical question, most likely not what he had planned to say. It just broke from him as I opened the door. "Do you realize what you've done?"

I asked him to come in and sit down. To retain my composure, I went to the kitchen and made tea, barely paying attention to his panicked chatter in the next room. Ihsan spoke a mile a minute; he was that keen to get away from a dangerous situation.

I brought in the tea, making myself walk as slowly as possible. Then I sat beside him and picked up his hand. I spoke gently but to the point.

"Ihsan, you live in those old poems you love so much. I know you try to love me as if I were in them too. How could I not be charmed?" I thought of Sumru and her favorite authors. "You live to read when it ought to be the other way around. But times have changed."

The situation had its comical side. He was scared, frightened of being found in my apartment; but male pride prevented him from admitting it. So I did it for him, and rather cruelly.

"I understand. You're afraid that because of me you'll lose your job-or worse."

He remonstrated, of course, claimed I had insulted him, that I had completely misconstrued things. Nevertheless, he was gone ten minutes later.

My parents phoned around dinner time. They had seen footage of the demonstration on the news. They had seen me. Their lyrics weren't the same as Ihsan's or Mr. Erkat's, but the tune was the same. There's a parapet, Veta; for God's sake keep your head below it.

I couldn't sit still, but I didn't want to go out on the streets. So, I was pacing my little apartment when the knock on the door came. It was a soft knock, almost tentative, a polite knock.

The fortyish man at my door was dressed in a business suit with a vest and a strikingly bright red tie. He was good-looking, prepossessing, and he never raised his voice. But he had a mustache that unsettled me. It was exactly like the president's.

He asked if he could speak with me. "Just for a short while, Veta." That he addressed me so familiarly, was creepy, like his mustache. He sat where Ihsan had and smiled at me, as Ihsan had not. He didn't give his name and I didn't ask. His manner was avuncular yet at the same time menacing.

"Look, Veta, we both know this isn't you. Yes, we both know it. You're a musician, a music teacher, not a political person at all. This petition of yours?" he scoffed. "And today's spectacle? I expect that cost you a good deal, didn't it? Of course it did. It's against your nature. Surely you know that you'll not only fail; you'll make yourself ridiculous. Give it up; go back to your life, to music, to the children."

There was no open threat. Had there been one I think the interview would have felt less sinister. He shook my hand, patted my shoulder, and left. I sat for an hour, outwardly tranquil, inwardly trembling, trying to decide what to do. I had to go to the bathroom twice. I put my disk of Ashkenazy playing the Études on the CD player. I fetched my passport, stuffed my knapsack, called my parents, hung up on my father, decided not to call my headmistress, went down to the street, and found a taxi to drive me to the airport. My credit card covered a one-way ticket to Paris where, if I'm not mistaken, Chopin composed Opus 10, no. 12, that wrathful paean to a crushed revolution.

My mind was vacant during the flight. I couldn't see beyond the back of the seat in front of me. When I got off the plane, I didn't know what to do or where to go. All airports resemble each other in being both somewhere and nowhere, functional as toaster-ovens. The place glared with fluorescent lighting. It was big and bustling but felt empty, as if all the people in it were ghosts. But, of course, I was the ghost, disconnected from everyone and everything.

I asked how to get a bus into the city. There I found a storefront that was just closing and exchanged all my cash for Euros. Then I looked for someplace cheap to get something filling-it was pasta-and found a room in a disreputable hotel and went right to sleep. I was exhausted.

The next morning, after coffee and a brioche, I bought a street map and took the Métro to the headquarters of the press organization Sumru had often mentioned approvingly. It was in an old building from the Belle Époque, but the inside looked as if it had been set up the day before. It was open plan with cubicles, computer screens, metal trays overflowing with folders, and dying house plants. The receptionist was a sleek young woman dressed in a stylish jet-black top and tight black jeans. She looked like a model or a cat burglar. I explained who I was and why I was there. She was polite but indifferent until I mentioned Sumru's name. That galvanized her. She took me at once to the Director's office, a quite disorderly one, as was its occupant, the formidable, busy, bald, beetle-browed Monsieur Henri Sayard. He knew all about what was going on back home. He knew a lot more than I did.

Monsieur Sayard began by asking after my accommodations. He held up a finger, made a call, and secured a decent hotel room for me. Then he offered me a coffee and listened patiently as I talked about Sumru. When I could say no more, I crossed my legs to indicate as much. Then he began what I suppose is called a debriefing. His questions were precise; my answers were not.

He nodded and rubbed his forehead. "Very well. The next thing is we'll want to hold a press conference. And as soon as possible. Tomorrow, in fact. Are you up to it?"

Well, was I?

I raised my chin. "Monsieur Sayard," I said, "why else should I be here?"

The offices included a conference room at the back. The receptionist took me to see the room in advance, so I could get the feel of the space. There was a plain wooden table, six blue chairs, and a good deal of empty floor. The far wall had three wide windows that looked out over a small garden with a round iron table and two curly chairs from which the white paint was flaking. They sat under a tree with red leaves.

The cat burglar pointed to the flimsy wall on the left side of the room. "It opens up," she said. "There's room for fifty people plus equipment." I asked her name. "I'm called Madeleine," she said. I thought momentarily of little girls in Catholic boarding schools, of Proust shot into the past. I fancied Madeleine must be like Sumru, a committed crusader, armed in self-conscious virtue and black denim. I wondered if my friend might have dressed that way had she chosen to go to London or Frankfurt. I went to the windows and stared into the garden. I thought of my gentleman-caller; its leaves were the same red color as his tie.

"That tree. Do you know what it is, what kind?"

Madeleine looked at me with French amusement. "A Japanese maple, I believe."

The press conference was to take place at mid-morning. The conference room had been opened up and was almost full when I arrived. The space, the seats, the people milling around-it all reminded me of recitals I had given; however, on this occasion I wouldn't be interpreting the scores of others but offering the audience my own words, an accounting and a plea. I'd hardly slept in the wide hotel bed. I kept thinking of that self-assured look above the telltale mustache. You will make yourself ridiculous. But, though I had to speak for myself, it was Sumru's tale I would tell, her plight, which stood for a more general one.

Overnight I wrote out a speech in longhand and in French. Now, the six pages of hotel stationery trembled in my hand. I reminded myself of Madeleine's instructions. "When the red light comes on, look straight at the camera. Monsieur Sayard will be seated beside you. He'll introduce you. Then you speak. You'll be expected to take questions."

"Do you think there will be any?"

Madeleine gave a little Gallic shrug, then wished me good luck and retreated to the back of the room.

After the press had gathered, Director Sayard didn't introduce me at once, as I'd expected. He spoke at length, first about his organization and its mission, then about the arrests in my country, the closed newspapers, the anger of journalists in France and everywhere, their professional solidarity, and their demands. At last, he got to me. I felt like an afterthought.

He mispronounced my name. Vita instead of Veta. Life.

I rose, lowered the microphone, and raised the pages of my speech. I'd have preferred a violin. I cleared my throat. The red light came on. It was brighter than the Japanese maple, than the tie. I believe my speech came off well enough. At least everybody was quiet while I read it. I was able to reply to the questions about Sumru. Monsieur Sayard answered the rest.

I've found work and an apartment in the 11th arrondissement. Twice each week I phone my parents. They say they miss me and I say the same.

There is still no word on Sumru's whereabouts.

Yesterday, I re-read Hamlet-not the whole of it, just Horatio's scenes. I always wondered about Horatio. Why, in a play with the most famous self-revealing soliloquies, did the Master feel the need to give the Prince a confidant? Horatio seems hardly more than that, a mere prop, like Gertrude's arras or Yorick's skull. A mannequin might have served as well. I couldn't make out what Shakespeare wanted with him. But this, after all, was Shakespeare-and at the acme of his powers. You've got to trust him.

The difference between a fine storyteller and a poor one is the reasons behind their choices. The good author is likely to have more than one reason, especially if you add the unconscious to the deliberate ones. Bad writers will likely have a single reason, and it will be perfectly transparent. For example, they may stick in a gratuitous romantic scene just to titillate readers or concoct a murder so improbably baroque in its complexity that the purpose is obviously to mystify, like an infuriatingly recherché clue in a crossword. Such stories are cheap and shallow. Shakespeare is neither and will have more than a single reason for his choices. Obviously, a play requires dialogue and Horatio is there for Hamlet to talk to; yet the prince's nature is so complex and varied that he never seems wholly disclosed even to himself. To what sort of person would Hamlet open his heart? Who would he choose as his best friend? Perhaps one reason Horatio's in the play is to answer these questions.

What do I know of Horatio? I know he is what Sumru thought me to be-equable, dispassionate, and logical-a Stoic in short. That's how Horatio sees himself at the end, calling himself "more an antique Roman than a Dane." He is a fatalist prepared to share the fate his friend has struggled against for five acts.

Except for keeping the secret of Hamlet's pretended madness and helping arrange for the production of The Murder of Gonzago, Horatio is detached from the action of the play, unentangled in the political intrigue. We hear nothing of his family, girlfriends, other pals. He has no official position at court and hardly interacts with anyone but Hamlet. He is the Prince's friend-his true and only one, nothing like the treacherous Rosencrantz and Guildenstern. Everybody ignores him. Yet he seems tied to the royal family. He was present when Hamlet Senior defeated the senior Fortinbras, and he is the one who explains about the old King's death. He has been studying alongside Hamlet at Wittenberg, and he is the first to learn of Hamlet's return from England. He's with the prince when he learns of Ophelia's death. Horatio is steady and skeptical. When applied to by the guards in Act One, he dismisses the Ghost as their "fantasy". His philosophy-if he's indeed a Stoic-is pantheistic, not supernatural. Of all the significant characters, Horatio alone survives the play's final massacre. He outlasts the tragedy but only to perform a service for his friend.

When Horatio loyally proposes finishing off the poison, Hamlet calls death "felicity" and the world "harsh" but begs his friend to defer the former and endure the latter. Hamlet's dissatisfaction with life and the world hasn't improved since "To be or not to be." Why would it when things have gone from bad to catastrophic, when he's dying surrounded by corpses and about to hand Denmark over to Fortinbras-Superman to his Clark Kent-undoing his father's work, incidentally. Hamlet's final words are addressed to his friend.

What is it about Horatio that so appeals to the Prince? Well, Hamlet tells us straight.   I wonder-did Sumru think the same of me?

> Since my dear soul was mistress of her choice
>
> And could of men distinguish, her election
> Hath seal'd thee for herself, for thou hast been
> A man that fortune's buffets and rewards
> Hast tak'n with equal thanks. . .
> > . . .Give me that man
> That is not passion's slave, and I will wear
> In my heart's core, ay, in my heart of heart,
> As I do thee.

So, why Horatio? Maybe there's a clue in his name. Horatio is a kind of amalgam of the Latin ratio and orator. Ratio. It is Horatio's imperturbable reasonableness that drew the more volatile prince, his composed acceptance of what comes without any of the resistance and whining in which the Hamlet indulges. And what of orator? This foretells the final charge imposed on Horatio by his dying friend, which is to preserve his own life and go sorrowfully into the world "to tell my story."

THE LAST PHILOSOPHER

Madam Chairman, members of the Organizing Committee of the annual Werner Kulm Conference, respected members of the Academy, and esteemed colleagues, I am profoundly honored by the invitation to deliver the keynote address to you this evening and will endeavor not to make it overlong.

You will appreciate that the title of my lecture is ironic. As yet, there has been no last philosopher, nor do I think there is likely to be one. I agree with Søren Kierkegaard who wrote that, humanly speaking, each generation must begin afresh. This means that we must not only learn for ourselves how to breathe and love and mourn and age but must take our own stabs at answering philosophy's perennial questions. Each generation begins by gnawing on the bones of its forebears, as Kierkegaard did on Hegel's. Perhaps what most irritated Kierkegaard about Hegel was that he was the sort of philosopher who really would have liked to be the last.

My lecture will be concerned with another pair of European thinkers. Naturally, my chief subject will be Werner Kulm but I will also have something to say about Karl Waisenhaus, who laid so relentlessly into Kulm's work.

According to his older sister's notes for an unpublished memoir, as a child Kulm was often solitary though seldom lonely. "During our years in the big house in Kaiserslachen," Charlotte writes,

> Werner's brightness prevented him from getting on with the other boys; he was impatient with them and they taunted him. Of girls he was frightened while grown-ups were frightened of him. Between the ages of seven and nine my brother kept company with the characters

of his marionette theater, a Christmas present from jolly Uncle Adalbert. Though Werner gave up in frustration after a few half-hearted attempts at making the puppets move, he liked to fashion costumes for them, with my help. He would sit them down or prop them up and stage conversations among them. Sometimes he pretended they were people we knew or figures from history like Frederick the Great and Bettina Brentano. At other times Werner cast the puppets as imaginary people with drolly pompous names such as the Graf Pharmacopia von Schwarzmastdarm.

With admirable understatement, Charlotte writes, "My brother was exceptionally advanced in his reading habits." She recalls happening on him in the nursery one afternoon as he conducted a dinner party for his puppets. He had placed four of them around a miniature table.

He used one of Father's handkerchiefs as a tablecloth. When I asked who the diners were, he pointed to each. 'That one's Bertrand Russell, she's Hildegard von Bingen, that fellow with the cottonwool beard is Martin Buber, and the good-looking lady over-that's Héloise, you know, from Peter Abelard.' So, it was boy-girl-boy-girl, modern-medieval-modern-medieval. 'Be quiet, Lotte. They're talking about God,' said my brother in that way he had even then of being solemn while making fun of me at the same time.

According to his sister, in later years Kulm dispensed with the marionettes, but continued to conduct what she calls "imaginary parliaments," with heated debates in strong language. Before their parents became accustomed to their son's habit of talking to himself in different voices, she says, they feared for Werner's sanity.

It seems to me that the exceptional comprehensiveness and profundity of Kulm's mature thought owes much to these childish symposia. It is as if he were able to be more than a single person, yet without ever ceasing to be Werner Kulm. Yes, I think that Kulm's greatness derives from this ability to be many people, to fashion, so to speak, a multifaceted mind, his unique e pluribus unum.

I hope you will pardon me if I now speak of some elementary matters.

There are only three kinds of questions in the world. First, there are ones like: when will this lecture be over or how old was Werner Kulm when he gave up playing with his puppet theater? These questions are about matters of fact, the kind historians and scientists investigate. They are called empirical questions after empeirikos, the Greek word for experienced, because they can be resolved by experiment or by experience. Do you prefer green or black olives? What color is an orange? Who won the Peloponnesian War? All these are empirical questions.

The second category of question is called formal. How much is two plus two? If the fielder catches a ball before it hits the ground is the batter out? If a Harvard language philosopher drives south from Boston at 55 mph while a deranged aesthetician from Brown heads north from Providence on the wrong side of Rte. 95 at 120 miles per hour, where will they meet up? You don't answer formal questions like these by watching baseball games, checking the historical record, or-Heaven forbid-by crashing cars; you get the answer by following certain pre-established rules, like those of logic, math, and baseball.

Now, of course there are clear methods for finding answers to empirical and formal questions. And if you can't find the answer on your own, you can usually track down an expert who can give it to you and show you why it's right.

This is not true of the third type of question, though: philosophical questions. Here it is not at all obvious how to find an answer nor even where to look for it. What is justice? How should people be governed? Is there a human nature? Is anything good-in-itself? How is it that we know things? What is the surest path to happiness? What is happiness?

Such questions are not pointless, not unanswerable; on the contrary, it is precisely because there are so many answers to such questions that it is easy to assert that none is final, even for the experts. Still, a multiplicity of answers is not enough of an explanation for philosophy's lack of conclusiveness. After all, I can conceive of an infinite number of answers to the questions of how much two plus two makes or who founded the Academy. All but four and Plato would be incorrect. So, is it really the case that no philosophical question can be finally and conclusively answered? And if so, why?

It might be argued that any question that can be finally answered would not be a philosophical one, that a philosophical question can be defined as one that cannot be finally answered. On the other hand, it could be said that only one thing is necessary to make a philosophical answer final: that everybody should accept that it is so. For most cultures at most periods this is, in fact, the case. Those who dissent are regulated by self-censorship, exile, re-education, ridicule, or martyrdom. The obvious riposte to this position is that such agreement, whether conventional or coerced, is limited by time and culture and that, anyway, conformity is not the same as conviction. Still, there is something unsatisfying in the tautological view that no philosophical question can be finally answered because if it is really a philosophical one then no answer can ever be accepted as final, except by those propounding it and perhaps not even by them.

So let us suppose something different, namely that philosophical questions are not conclusively answered because we don't want them to be. If it were a matter of a medical diagnosis the opposite would be true. Too many answers to the question, "What's wrong with me,

Doctor?" are as good as none at all. But with philosophical questions the opposite seems to be true; a single answer, delivered with certainty and finality, makes us suspicious and provokes rebuttals and objections. It would be surprising if the philosophers who supply such answers did not themselves know that, while their answers must be presented as final, they will not be final. Even the relativists, who might be expected to proclaim the provisional nature of their relativism ("it suits our times" or "this is just the way things seem to me now, at ten a.m. on Tuesday morning")-even the relativists sound absolute about their relativism.

If there is such a thing as a weariness with philosophy's inconclusiveness, a taedium philosophiae, then it may have reached its zenith with the Vienna Circle and the natural language philosophers of the early twentieth century. In their respective ways, these exasperating or exasperated thinkers tried to draw a line under old-fashioned philosophical speculation, annihilating philosophical questions simply by declaring them meaningless. And why if not because they are incapable of being answered with finality? Of course, they failed because their arguments, intended to put an end to philosophical argument, ironically became just another episode in the long argument that is the history of philosophy, no more final than what they attacked for not being final. Worse, they began the growth of a new branch on the tree they meant to cut down, filling up the professional journals and the minds of graduate students with the speculations of a new meta-philosophy.

Nevertheless, many people, even those who are not graduate students or professional philosophers, are dismissive of philosophy on the ground that any answer to a philosophical question is no more than a matter of opinion, relative to the point of pointlessness, perhaps important to the individual who delivers it -on the one hand irrefutable, on the other unverifiable. Nevertheless, our species devotes a lot of attention and considerable prestige to philosophizing and grants the status of great philosopher to few human beings, to far fewer than, say, poets, musicians, or athletes. This would be odd if the answers to philosophical questions really had no importance, no practical worth. But they do have such importance and worth. To live, we human beings require at least provisional notions about ethics, government, friendship, knowledge, logic, and aesthetics. It seems to me that thinkers, cultures, and eras are not distinguished so much by posing novel philosophical questions as by embracing new answers to perennial ones.

No, the simplest hypothesis is the best: people do not want final answers to philosophical questions. And by people I mean philosophers. One might almost think that what is essential to them is not the triumph of their own ideas-though they certainly write that way -but that the conversation continue.

Picture a great philosopher, another Aristotle or Kant, one who has answered all philosophical questions not only to his own satisfaction but to that of nearly everybody else. How long would it take such a genius to feel this comprehensive triumph as a catastrophe? How would he respond as he watched the discipline he loved wither before his eyes and because of him?

This brings me back to our subject because I submit that Werner Kulm was just that philosopher. Another Kant, a latter-day Aristotle-these are the epithets and comparisons he actually evoked from his contemporaries. How would Kulm have reacted to such a situation? How would the man who spent his childhood years putting clashing views into the mouths his puppets have responded if not dialectically? The needful thing to him, I submit, would have been to undermine his own victory, to do what none of his contemporaries was capable of doing with any success, which was to question the brilliant and convincing answers to the questions of philosophy given by Werner Kulm.

You might say that, even if I am right, Kulm could simply have chosen to revise his ideas, but re-pointing the bricks only confirms the structure that is already there. What Kulm would have wanted was a wrecking-ball. And since the questions he answered to everyone's satisfaction really were philosophical ones, this would not have been hard for him to do. The only surprising and unprecedented thing is that he should have to do it himself, philosophers being, if you will pardon me for saying so, notoriously contentious, envious, and disagreeable people. Yet had Kulm at the end of his career attacked his own ideas this would have caused consternation, raising the suspicion that he had been playing games all along or, worse yet, that the certainties on which his contemporaries were blithely proceeding with their lives and the finality for which they had thanked him with forty-three honorary degrees and a national medal, by attaching his name to five boulevards, three comprehensive polytechnics, two parks and one frigate was just a cruel illusion. People would be justifiably indignant with him if they thought Kulm had compelled their belief in his ideas without believing them himself. That sort of thing leaves people feeling foolish and cheated and with no way to regard their ex-master except as a confidence trickster.

There is also Kulm's vanity to consider, the fulfillment of his ambition. After all, his name had become an established adjective and remains so to this day: Kulmian minimalist logic, the Kulmian maximalist imperative, Kulmian analytics and dynamic method, etc. He who had set out with the hope of someday being among the philosophers-as Keats wished to be among the English poets-had superseded them all. But at what price? He had done what Wilde claimed all men do; he had killed the thing he loved. What Kulm had killed was love itself, philosophia, the love of wisdom, because what is finished really is dead, even should it be as perfect as a diamond.

And so, I submit that Kulm did the logical thing. He invented a pseudonym, a puppet, to demolish his own ideas. I like to imagine it was with joy and relish that he reversed his initials and wrote as the obscure and parentless Karl Waisenhaus. In the series of critical articles with which you are all familiar, inventive vituperation and self-mockery erupted like hot lava to flow over the whole terrain of Kulm's life's work. As Waisenhaus, his last marionette, he opened all the doors he had with astonishing brilliance and infinite pains closed, as Kulm. He must have felt like the heroes of the old Westerns who, having established law and order, turn their horses' heads toward the setting sun and the lawless frontier. Love, he would have thought to himself, is more verb than noun, philosophy a thing you do over and over rather than a doctrine you have once and for all.

As you know, I am the official editor of Kulm's papers. Among them, I found a sort of preface attached to offprints of the first five articles of Karl Waisenhaus. It is written in Kulm's own hand and begins with this sentence: "I will make him twenty-five years my junior, fierce and unrestrained, a hungry lion keen to devour my flesh and gnaw on my bones."

Thank you all for your attention.

LEDA LIEBLING

Dear Ms. Schrader,

Thank you for allowing us to choose our own topics for the last paper assignment this semester. I have chosen to write about the singer-songwriter Leda Liebling. I looked up everything published about Ms. Liebling in English and French and-with some effort and a great deal of luck-conducted one short interview.

Leda Liebling is regarded as a mysterious figure, aloof and solitary. For a few months, she got a lot of attention after the release of her first album. It was widely played and favorably reviewed. Magazine articles were written about her, and photographs of her were all over the Internet. Then she suddenly seemed almost to vanish.

Why am I interested in Leda Liebling? Her early songs helped me through my junior year in high school when some bad things were going on around me, in me as well. This debt, along with Ms. Liebling's integrity and disdain for celebrity are what prompted me to seize the opportunity of this assignment to find out more about her.

I hope it will be all right that my essay is not a formal research paper. You didn't stipulate that was what you wanted. I hope you will like what I have written at least a little.

Thank you for your enlightening course.

Phyllis

Phyllis Lamontaine

English 102, Ms. Schrader

LEDA LIEBLING ALONE: ARTIST AND SURVIVOR

Part One: Things Almost Everybody Knows

Three years ago, Leda Liebling's album Laurels scored, as they say, a critical and popular success. The lyrics are serious, even tragic, but the melodies are either catchy or gorgeous, some make you think of a circus, others of couples waltzing. Her guitar playing was often compared to James Taylor's.

The story goes that Leda Liebling was performing in some small L.A. club when a record company executive discovered her, gave her a studio, a contract, a back-up band, and promotion. This makes a good story, though hardly an original one, especially in Los Angeles, the city with the largest population of hopeful, not-yet-discovered stars. Even if people knew it was a fairy tale, they bought it because the story fit the grooves and there was no reason to question it. I know I was more interested in the songs and the songwriter than whatever machinations led to my hearing them. The funny thing is that the tale is apparently true, or at least mostly true.

Laurels had a lot of pain and bitterness in its lyrics, and I guess it caught the mood of girls around my age—too old for 'tween pop, too young for brutal hip-hop, too suburban for club music, too cool for retro ballads. To me, the anguish in the lyrics was glamorous. If they bothered to listen to the songs on Laurels, parents were, like mine, satisfyingly horrified.

Messed and marked and mucked up,
Fouled confused and fucked up;

Yet she's got such pretty hair,
such long and silken hair. . .

Some songs were disturbing even to me because they confirmed my apprehensions about the world and myself-my worst suspicions. Laurels seemed to embody a compelling, if obscure, wisdom. Leda could write the sort of lines you turn over and over when you can't sleep, when everything is quiet and you are alone.

Remember, when you lie down to rest,
Your worst is better than your best.

Other songs spoke directly to girls like me, fixed the texture of our teenage lives, our schools, our confused sexual attraction/repulsions. Take these lines from "Harding High" for example:

The nice boys are too weak
The strong ones aren't nice.
Boys are an infestation
Just like bed bugs and lice.

My schedule is a sentence.
The moment they ring the bell
The halls are packed with sinners.
Harding's all nine circles of Hell.

After Laurels took off, the media went after Leda Liebling. There were biographical articles-mostly vapid or made-up-and all those photo-shoots. Still, Leda granted no interviews and gave no concerts. She did perform one song as the musical guest on SNL then-nothing. Demand was higher than ever, but Leda adamantly supplied nothing. The story had it she was a recluse. Comparisons were made to Greta Garbo (I looked her up - I vant to be alone). By refusing celebrity Leda became an object of mystery. She was different. To young fans like me, her turning her back, even on us, looked like integrity, authenticity. We took it as disgust with the phony media machine, of which we, too, wanted to believe we had had enough. Not caring about money was a further proof of genuineness. For a time, indifference to fame became cool, fashionable. Young women imitated her, at least the superficial things they knew of her. They wore tight black jeans and cowboy boots, let their hair grow long-even dyed it jet black-cultivated aloofness and a morose solitude. According to one tabloid article, which might have been pure fabrication, Leda Liebling did not even date. As to fame, she was famously quoted as asking, "Why would I want to be known by people I don't want to know?" But some reporter may have made that up.

Eventually the talk show producers stopped phoning and the paparazzi went elsewhere. The record company canceled her contract for a second album.

I understand why the vogue for Leda Liebling could not last long. For one thing, she was independently wealthy, a quality harder to imitate than her Johnny Cashesque outfits. Her fans might have admired her anti-sociability, but they didn't really share it. It's only possible to be cool in the sight of others. Solitude isn't so cool if nobody's there to notice it.

I read somewhere that most vices are social and most virtues personal. Leda Liebling seemed to me to possess a lot of personal virtue and the proof was that she isolated herself when she didn't have to. I liked that she stuck to what was essential and genuine: just herself, her guitar, and her songs.

It didn't take long before another mega-hit came along, sung by a performer more accommodating to and cooperative with the media, a singer-songwriter who was more sentimental and easier to understand than Leda Liebling.

Part Two: Things Hardly Anybody Knows

Leda was born Leda Sylvia Lehman in Santa Barbara, California, and raised there. She had an older sister, Daphne. Her mother was fond of the Greek myths. Leda was born six years younger than her sister. She was thirteen when Daphne died.

The mythical Daphne, of course, escaped Apollo when her father turned her into a laurel tree. Some critics speculated Leda called her album Laurels to suggest victory, a championship, seeing in it an act of bravado, even hubris. The title song is actually about her sister; in fact, the entire album is about Daphne's suicide.

The key of the title song is B-minor, the one in which Bach set his mass (BWV 232) and Scarlatti the most profound of his sonatas (K. 87). The melody, though, is not lugubrious. It sounds like a transposition into the minor of something jollier, something that used to be in the major-that is, a tune that was once happy.

"Laurels" was Leda's nickname for her big sister, whom she adored. Daphne called her "Eggs."

In the bleak reaches of the night
Wrong gets all mixed up with right,
Despair's more plausible than hope,
Especially when you're out of dope.
And so she took a razor blade-
Deep, deep the two cuts that she made;
Red the trickle and red the gush.
She heaved one sigh then she hushed.

It's no go, no go, you know.
Killed by an asshole or by blow;
No go restlessness, no go rest.
Oblivion is all that's left.

The Lehman family was blown up by Daphne's suicide. Leda's parents stood guilty before one another, accused each other, briefly offered some clumsy comfort to Leda but soon ignored her in favor of clawing at one another. When they divorced, Leda stayed with her mother and visited with her father on weekends. She was equally unhappy with both. Her father was a big shot in one of the larger production companies. Three months after the divorce was final, he remarried. Leda disliked his second wife-a young actress she nicknamed The Cliché. When her father and the The Cliché were killed in a private plane crash on their way to Montana to look at a ranch they planned to buy Leda became rich. She was seventeen. That was when she changed her name, dropped out of school, moved into an apartment in Los Angeles, and began writing songs.

I found some of this out from an interview in a now-defunct French music magazine, Musique de Jeunesse. The interview was not with Leda but with the executive who had signed her. The contract for the second album had just been canceled. I imagine he was feeling disappointed, angry, maybe betrayed. Perhaps that's why he spilled so many beans. The rest I discovered from public records but mostly from a conversation with the singer herself.

Leda Liebling, even if she is a recluse, has many and varied interests. She is a cyclist and collector of antique mantel clocks. She has also published two articles on the poetry of Gene Derwood (1909-1954). I can see why Leda found the poet sympathetic. Derwood wrote religious poems that are short on religious consolation:

. . . Grow mild before the flicking lash
seems welded to your hand, self-wounder. . .
No seeded faith before, nor after, miracle,
Of bidden faith in things unseen, no particle.
For we think only through our troubled selves.

No one should be surprised that a singer-songwriter writes autobiographically. It has been the lyric tradition, from Sappho to Taylor Swift. Nevertheless, nobody seems to have looked closely into how autobiographical Leda's first album was; I mean the specifics. Maybe this was because of Leda's manner-the scorn of self-promotion, the nearly haughty silence, those armor-like black jeans. Everyone knew the songs had to come from somewhere, of course, and that this somewhere had to be Leda's life; all the same they (we, I) saw them in an abstract light, as universal rather than personal. I believe it was because Laurels seemed autobiographical in general that girls like me felt themselves read by it, moved even by the elusive wisdom of "Gnomic Song":

Arcanae in roots of heather,
chthonous rumbling under clods:
if gods didn't make the weather,
surely weather made the gods.

Go pluck pits from brittle pods,
songs from lungs fretted with feather.
If weather hasn't made the gods,
Surely gods have made the weather.

From the French article I learned that Leda is also an amateur astronomer (myths in the heavens) and a geocacher. I am also into geocaching, and I came across the name Leda Lehman and her email address in a newsletter. She was cited as the chief organizer in a northern California district. Geocaching is a treasure-hunting game. Players use GPS devices, guiding themselves to specific locations where they try to uncover concealed containers. The hiding of the containers and maintenance of the sites are done by the most devoted members of the community, like Leda. Just before Spring Break, I succeeded in connecting with Leda by email and somehow convinced her to take me along on a hunt. I would have been ashamed to trick her. I told her I knew that she was Leda Liebling and admitted I was a fan but stressed my enthusiasm for geocaching. To my amazement, she agreed to let me join her and suggested a specific day, the Tuesday of spring break, and a place up in Mendocino. I booked a night at the Holiday Inn in Fort Brag and borrowed a car.

We rendezvoused at the trailhead at eight in the morning. Leda Liebling is tall, reserved, and as charismatic as ever. She was wearing blue jeans, a sweatshirt, and her hair was a little shorter than it used to be.

"How long have you been at it?" she asked. "Geocaching I mean."

"Oh, I'm still pretty new. Only a year and only on vacations. I've been out just four times, actually."

She was so nice to me, told me about the tricks of camouflaging. "Always check the trees." About half an hour in she began asking me about myself, about school, my family, my plans. I answered all her questions; in fact, I probably went on a little too long. Then I told her that Laurels was my favorite album of all time and about the bad things it had gotten me through.

"You may have saved my life," I said dramatically. It was only as I spoke the words that I realized how true they were.

And that seems to have pried open the door. Not all at once, but in short snatches through the morning Leda revealed some details about her life and her family.

"Do you still write songs?" I asked.

She laughed. "Writing songs is a serious hobby; that is, a habit, a disease."

We talked a little about things the critics had said about her work. I observed that the consensus was that she was a Romantic.

She scoffed. "Beethoven said only the pure in heart can make a good soup. That's Romanticism for you. Do you think I'm a Romantic?"

It was a wonderful experience being with her, and all too brief. We found the cache and walked back to the trailhead where I thanked her and we said goodbye. Two weeks later, I got an email from Leda with an attachment. It was an MP3 of a new song. She said she was sending it to me because it was our morning together that had inspired it.

"It's been a long time since I spoke to anybody about my family. In fact, I don't talk to anybody about them. I don't know why but it felt good talking to you."

The title of the song is "Black Forest Cake." The melody is tender; here are the lyrics:

Hansel and Gretel needed a mother,
Lost a good one but got another.
Rock candy just wasn't the same-
What was that old witch's name?
Was it mother, Mother?

Gretel and Hansel had a weak father,
Married a bitch and just wouldn't bother.
Could he really not have seen
How greedy she was, how cruel, how mean?
Who was that feckless father, Father?

What the kids found instead of love
Were chocolate walls and a Topf stove.
All the same, the two survived,
Took the treasure, then they thrived.
Clever girl, resourceful lad,
Screwed-up mom, worthless dad.

Note: J. A. Topf und Söhne was the company that manufactured the furnaces used by the Nazis in their death camps.

SUITE POPULAIRE AMÉRICAINE

1.

After four days of enervating July mugginess pumped up from the swamps of Dixie, the air felt dry and light. The two-lane blacktop was nearly free of traffic and, though there wasn't even much wind to fight, Joseph Tritto pedaled hard. Six days earlier his affair with Joyce Kleinschmidt had ended abruptly when, to his own astonishment, he clearly declared into his phone, "I can't do this anymore." He had no intention of saying any such thing yet it popped out of him and so it must have been seething inside, down below, like magma: disappointment, humiliation, the unacknowledged calculation that their relationship had flipped from being a source of pleasure and hope to one of pain and grief. I can't do this anymore. He wasn't even sure whether this referred to the affair itself or just his asking when he would see her, which is what he had just been doing. "He's out of town for two days. You told me yourself." Joseph noted the whining tone and was exasperated by it. And Joyce said nothing. Joyce was silent. That was what had provoked the eruption. No matter how hard he pedaled, how fast he went, he still heard that silence, loud as the gap on Nixon's tape. The silence proved that, though he might be surprised by what he'd said, she wasn't; and it occurred to him that she'd just been waiting for him to catch on and end things. She didn't exert herself to change his mind, to ask him to specify what this was. She didn't ask for an explanation at all, let alone to see him. What she did say after a good ten seconds of nothing was, "Please don't send me any letters. Or emails." Once she'd cherished his notes to her, all beginning MDSJ, for "my dear sweet Joyce." When had they become unwelcome, annoying? Or did she fear an analysis that would wring her heart? Joseph was the poet/shrink of the pair; he was the one who liked to talk about feelings, who took the temperature of the thing that was this. Was it womanly of him? Was that the problem? Anyway, those ten Mississippies of silence brought on the unexpected finale. The remaining ambiguity was that he couldn't decide if he had chosen to end it or if he had been manipulated into doing it. Was a break what she wanted but lacked the courage to ask? Was tricking him into bringing down the cleaver a way of claiming the high ground, plausible denial, exculpation? It only made things worse to know that she could have had him back at any time. For days, he waited expectantly for a phone call, obsessively checked email. He fantasized about a desperate call at midnight, about her showing up at his apartment drenched in tears, the arrival of a long, handwritten letter full of the love that, he had to admit, she'd never really expressed-the closest she'd come was at the start, when she'd called him "my best friend." Yes, even a businesslike email would have summoned him back, the brusquest of text messages. But the silence persisted like a bitter February.

Joseph had told no one of the affair, but for a time had considered confiding in his friend Patrick. He didn't want advice but merely the relief of speech. It was a dishonorable impulse, and he was glad he hadn't given in to it. Patrick always spoke of women with the unromantic authority of a gay man. He reminded Joseph of Chamfort's aphorism: "one must choose between loving women and understanding them." Patrick would have savored such a conversation with Joseph; he would have turned it into a monologue, half-sermon, half-case study. Then it occurred to Joseph that Patrick, a colleague who had often seen him and Joyce together, would almost certainly have figured out they were having an affair. A second-rate violinist but a gifted teacher, Patrick Casillas was one of those on whom nothing is lost, even if he sometimes had to invent things not to lose. He would have picked up on an exchanged look, a touch, a gesture. The surprising thing was that he had never said anything about it; Patrick enjoyed gossiping to people's faces even more than behind their backs.

Joseph was depressed. He stopped working. His muse was gone. And there was work that needed to be done, a deadline barely a month off. Unlike his defunct affair, which had led to nothing, this work stood to be consequential. The previous year he had composed a piece he called Petite Suite Populaire for two pianos. It had begun as a jeu d'esprit written for two of the Conservatory's advanced students. They were charming and ferociously diligent girls, one from Colombia, the other a first-generation Chinese-American. They were so serious about music that Joseph wanted to loosen them up. Up till now his composing had also been serious to a fault, so the levity of the Suite was good for him as well. The conductor of the city's philharmonic had attended the Conservatory's year-end recital and was taken with the piece. He liked it so much that he commissioned an orchestral version to be performed at the first concert of the new season in September. "Perhaps," he said in his punctilious Belgian accent, "I will place it last and leave them happy-non! I think first. But then again, maybe last. We shall make everybody happy first." The title Suite Populaire came from Villa-Lobos, but it was chiefly the anti-Wagnerian spirit of the French composers known as Les Six, that inspired him. It was a kind of music-sweet and acerbic by turns-that people liked hearing, which couldn't be said of his prior work. It might even earn him a name. While he was writing it, he felt elated, almost light-headed; it was like crossing from a dark room into a well-lit one, from ponderous to buoyant, from Deutschland to La France. But now the orchestration, like his life, had stalled. Maybe it was being blocked that made him yearn for a long bike ride, to go well beyond his usual route, far into the exurbs, as if by some magic he would regain momentum by pedaling himself to exhaustion.

He passed pines, stands of birch, some beech trees and water meadows. As he coasted by a horse farm, he smiled to think how far out he was. There were huge houses concealed behind evergreens and set well back from the road. Many had circular driveways and iron gates set in fieldstone walls. He pedaled by ponds and through picturesque town centers with clapboard churches, Civil War monuments, and police headquarters housed in old taverns. He passed new developments too, super-sized colonials and capes that looked like steroidal impostors set among two-hundred-year-old homesteads with weathered shingles and sensible proportions.

Joseph let his mind pass randomly from Joyce, to Patrick, to the Suite and what to do with woodwinds, strings, and brass. He was in a groove and when he came on a quick, steep hill, he scorned to downshift, rose from the saddle, and hammered up the blind rise. He didn't anticipate the mound of road sand that had been pushed into the declivity on the other side and just plowed into it. There was no slow motion. On the contrary, everything happened in an instant. The front wheel of his Univega crunched into the soft sand and stopped; the rear wheel lifted, the pedals fell from his feet, his body lurched and tumbled-suddenly airborne then violently not; he wasn't sure of the physics. Stupefied, he found himself on the pavement. His helmet was knocked sideways. His head hurt some and his right arm more. He staggered to his feet and got out of the road. Had the SUV and dump truck that that had whizzed by him just before he took the hill been behind him, he'd certainly have been dead or mangled. "I'll have to bike home" was his first thought. He had no money, no wallet or phone. The handlebars were askew and so was the front wheel. "If I did have a phone, would I call her?" he wondered then noticed the blood and searched for the source, which turned out to be gritty abrasions, the deepest to his left shoulder and right elbow.

Through the trees across the road, he made out the turret of a Victorian house. Maybe someone would be home and he could get help, at least make a call. Patrick would come for him in his little Honda, if he could get him on the phone.

Joseph's right arm hurt most when it hung down, a little less when bent, so he held his right wrist up with his left hand. "Must have broken something," he thought in a detached way, as if his arm were not part of him at all, just a burden he had to carry. He wrangled the bike into the high weeds at the side of the road, tossed his dented helmet, then made for the house.

The entrance to the driveway was marked by two fieldstone pillars, one with the street number set in it. A new black Mercedes sedan and a white Lexus were parked at the end of the driveway in front of a garage big enough to hold a trio of Abrams tanks. The driveway snaked through an expanse of weedless lawn. The house itself was an appealing pile, old-fashioned but renovated with four new skylights. It reminded him of his sister's doll house. Rhododendron bushes, spirea, day lilies, and giant hosta grew below the porch. A privet hedge, trimmed flat as a runway, stretched from one side of the house down to the woods where he guessed there was a stream. "This is what Patrick means by Plutopia," Joseph thought, focusing on his surroundings to prove to himself he could, that he wasn't in shock. His legs felt a little wobbly.

The front door was imposing, dark oak and stained glass. The long windows on either side were open, and Joseph was about to ring the bell when he heard a man's raised voice. A line from Shakespeare popped into Joseph's not altogether clear mind: I understand the fury in your words but not your words. He stepped back from the door and crept along the porch to the open window on the left. It was so bright outside that it was took him a moment to see inside. A young woman in jeans and a white peasant blouse was standing behind a couch on which sat an older woman in a tennis dress. A few feet away, just on the other side of a glassy coffee table, an agitated man in a business suit was yelling. Joseph heard him say, "I'm going to kill you first-I'll kill all of you!" Then he saw the pistol. The man wasn't pointing it at anybody, just holding it at his left side where it swung like a pendulum as he put his strength into screaming a string of men's names, places, dates, and insults.

The next five minutes were dreamlike, full of action unencumbered by thought. Joseph made his way as quietly as he could to the rear of the house. He found a pile of wood behind the garage, firewood but also lengths of lumber and fence palings. With his left hand-he no longer felt so much pain in his right arm but he knew that it was swelling-

he chose a piece of split hardwood that was roughly bat-sized. The rear door had been left open to let in the fresh air. He slowly opened the screen door and stole into an immense kitchen, with granite counters, a butcher block, and about a dozen hanging copper pans that made him think of a pipe organ. The voice was clearer now. He had apparently finished delivering his catalogue of infidelities. "For years I've put up with your shit and you fucking want a divorce? You bitch!"

Joseph tiptoed down a passageway. He could see into the living room now, but no one spotted him. The man was raising the pistol. There was a kind of scream-definitely a scream, yet a soft one, a scream riding an indrawn breath. Joseph made his move. He leapt into the room. The man began to turn toward him, his face red, amazed, the gray gun still pointed at the women.

Joseph swung his club at the man's left arm, the one with the gun at the end of it. It was an upward stroke aimed at the elbow so if the pistol went off it would miss the women. But the blow was too light; the gun didn't go off. The man fumbled with the thing but managed to hold on to it. Joseph aimed his second blow against the side of the man's head. He went down and the gun skittered under the coffee table. The woman in the tennis dress leaned down-casually, it seemed to Joseph, almost with indifference-and picked it up by the barrel. The man was not unconscious. He groaned, drew up his legs, his hands holding both sides of his head, like the figure in Munch's Scream. Blood seeped from his ear.

The next minutes were blurred. Joseph felt suddenly cold and fuddled. Later, he recalled collapsing into an armchair and the young woman dashing to the kitchen where she apparently called 911. To Joseph it seemed the police were there in seconds, as if they had been waiting outside all along, peering curiously through the windows, waiting to see what he would do.

2.

The air had been filled with sirens, the driveway with official vehicles-two police cars, one van, a couple of ambulances, and a fire truck. The pistol was bagged, its owner handcuffed, his head treated; then he was hustled off in one of the ambulances, guarded by two local policemen, for whom this was clearly an Event. The EMTs put a temporary splint on Joseph's right arm, cleaned his abrasions, then waited patiently as his throbbing arm blew up to Popeye proportions. A detective in a blue blazer took his statement. The detective looked as if he might have had his lunch at the country club interrupted. He was evenly tanned; his glossy hair was nicely parted. "Just a preliminary statement, Mr. Tritto," he said suavely. "Or is it Professor? Yes? Well, we'll be wanting to see you again, of course; but for now. . ." The woman Joseph decided must be the wife sat at the dining room table talking quietly with a cop in uniform. Joseph was struck by the calm with which she spoke to the policeman, just as he had been by the casual way she had picked up the gun. The young woman he decided must be a daughter. Her statement was being taken in the kitchen by a policewoman. He could just hear the tone of her voice. It was agitated, certainly, even emotional, but under control, the way Martha Argerich played Chopin.

As the EMTs were escorting Joseph toward the front door, the daughter dashed into the living room, saying over her shoulder-whether to the policewoman or her mother wasn't clear-that she was going to go with him, with Joseph, that she would follow the ambulance, wait at the hospital, then drive him home. Nobody offered any objection which Joseph found surprising. "Not necessary," he mumbled, feeling guilty, as if he too were being led away in cuffs. Was she grateful or angry? After all, the only physical violence that had occurred was committed by him and against her father.

It crossed Joseph's mind that Joyce's husband also might be capable of murderous rage. Had he become suspicious? Had Joyce been threatened? Joseph couldn't prevent feeling some sympathy for the man he had attacked. He had been shattered by Joyce's rejection; that he too could be driven to frenzy wasn't beyond contemplating. And what had he been feeling when he leapt into the living room like a one-armed Baryshnikov? Except for a couple childhood brawls, he had never hit anyone-certainly not the way he had the man he now knew was named Banister. With so many reasons to feel guilty, it never occurred to him to look for thanks. In fact, the women had said nothing at all to him, and he thought the dapper detective had looked suspicious. On the cop shows, the detectives always said they mistrusted coincidences.

One of the EMTs moved aside and the young woman was beside him. "I know who you are," she said.

"Of course. You heard me give my name to the police."

"No. I mean I know who you are, what you do. I've seen you on stage. You weren't wearing shorts and a T-shirt then. Or a sling. I heard both your symphony and your Suite Populaire."

He wasn't displeased. "I suppose you preferred the suite, like everybody else."

"With respect, Mr. Tritto, you're the one who chose the title."

"True."

"I also know two of your former students." She gave their names, both female. Joseph thought that this was far too much coincidence for any detective, even one with a snug berth in placid Plutopia instead of network TV.

They spent a full hour at the nice suburban hospital. She brought him a tuna sandwich and an iced tea while he waited to be released. Then they were in the Lexus, driving not to his apartment but back to her house. The doctor said Joseph had probably suffered some shock as well as a slight concussion and it would be preferable for him not to be left alone for twenty-four hours. "Do you live alone?" she asked and when he admitted he did, she said, "In that case, you're coming with me." He demurred, of course. "Just to be on the safe side," she insisted. "And don't waste your breath. I'm not taking no for an answer. And I'm a good violinist."

He had to wait with an orderly while she retrieved the car. When he got in, Joseph asked, "If I've got a broken arm and a concussion, what does your father have?" He was not trying to be amusing; on the contrary, he really was afraid he had shattered Banister's elbow and fractured his skull. He had certainly tried to.

She shook her head.

"I checked with the doctor who looked him over. Broken eardrum, some ruptured capillaries. No big deal, he said. Arm's fine, just bruised. Cranial x-ray negative." He wondered if her lack of affect was normal. She hadn't sounded so detached when giving her statement to the police. He examined her profile and saw that it was a charming one; he also noted the color of her hair and liked it. Odd that he had taken in so much about the house, the landscape, the plants, but hardly anything about the people. He was also surprised that she looked familiar.

"Holly Banister?" he said slowly, his voice mimicking the speed of his sluggish brain. "I know the name. In fact, I've seen you too. You played with the Manfredi Quartet last year. Schubert."

"And Shostakovich. My sister's better on the flute than I am on either the viola or the fiddle."

"Your sister?"

"Hadley. Holly and Hadley. And mother's Heidi. Can you believe it?" She made a sour face at the windshield. "Hadley just turned seventeen. She's up at the White Mountains festival, thank God. I'll have to call her. She's going to insist on coming home. What a mess."

Joseph was replaying the scene in the living room. "Did he, your father I mean-was all that. . . sudden?"

"Sudden? Depends on what you mean by sudden. The gun was sudden, but the jealousy and the vituperation weren't. I guess my mother asking him for a divorce was sudden, but I'd also say it was inevitable. She told him this morning, apparently. So, I guess it wasn't sudden and yet it was. It can take a long time for a thing to suddenly become sudden."

Joseph thought of Joyce and of how long she must have waited for him to catch on.

"How long had he been going on like that? I mean the shouting and the gun."

"Nearly half an hour, I think, though it felt like a month, which is why I didn't believe he'd actually shoot us. But the police said the gun was loaded. A full clip, they said." She twisted in the seat. "Why don't you tell me about your bike accident? Arm hurting less since they set it?"

"Well, that and the Ibuprofen." Joseph became self-conscious, looked down at his bare legs, felt the dried sweat encasing him. "Wish I had some proper clothes."

"We can stop and buy some."

"I don't have my wallet. I'm right-handed," he added irrelevantly.

"Then you're going to have a hard time with zippers."

He was pleased that she teased him. All he could think to say was, "But I need to write."

"People manage. They get used to using the other hand."

"I haven't got time." He explained about the commission, the deadline, admitted he was stalled but didn't say why.

"I could help you with that," she said just as flatly as she said everything else. "I might even be capable of having ideas."

They rode in silence for half a mile or so. Then Holly said, "Want to hear something funny?"

For a moment he thought she was going to tell a joke, maybe something about zippers, as if her world had not just been detonated and her life nearly lost.

"Funny?"

"I was engaged to be married. I broke it off. Yesterday. Coincidences come in pairs."

Joseph sighed. "I'm sorry. Is it proper to say I'm sorry?"

"I think it's one of those rare occasions when sympathy and congratulations both work."

"And neither does any good. I suppose you're off men, then."

"Off marriage, I'd say."

Again, his mouth outran his mind. "Good." He spoke too quickly, meaning to cancel what she'd just said by seconding it, and this was because he was attracted to her but hadn't yet realized it. But now they both did.

After that Holly fell silent but her silence was only superficially like Joyce's. To Joseph, it sounded entirely different.

3.

Holly and Joseph found Heidi Banister in the kitchen making chocolate chip cookies. Left alone, she had changed into a low-cut red sundress.

Holly explained why she had brought Joseph back, though her mother expressed neither curiosity nor surprise on seeing him. Still, he felt a bit like a big, wrongly delivered package. Heidi rubbed her hands on a dish towel, grinned at her daughter, and pointed at the bowl full of chocolate studded batter.

"You loved it this way when you were little."

Holly stuck in a finger and said to Joseph, "Apparently making cookies is what you do when your husband goes crazy and somebody falls from the sky and brains him."

"So?" asked Heidi.

Holly informed her mother perfunctorily. "He's okay, nothing broken. Mm, I do love your cookies," she said like a little girl, dropping the Lexus keys on the polished granite and scooping up a second finger's worth of batter.

Joseph had the sense that neither of them knew how to conduct themselves-not with him, not with each other. But, whatever they were feeling, it wasn't hysterical-at least not yet.

Heidi Banister nodded at his arm in its sling. "So, you did all that with a broken arm?"

"I want to apologize," Joseph started to say, not knowing himself what he should apologize for-coming in without ringing the bell, smashing her husband's arm and head, being brought back by Holly, wearing shorts and smelling like a cyclist, for overhearing her husband's rant? Heidi stopped him by saying something uncanny.

She waved her hand as if brushing away a gnat. "Apologize away. Wallow in it, if you want."

After that, he didn't want to apologize at all.

"Did you phone Hadley?" Holly asked.

"I could say I forgot but I'm putting it off," her mother replied, as she spooned a dollop of batter onto the cookie sheet. "What I actually forgot was to preheat the oven."

"We have to call her.'"

"Naturally. Will you do it, please?"

Holly threw Joseph an "I-told-you-so" look. It was a significant moment. The most complicit communication between people is always wordless. There are looks that make a bond, or confirm one.

"Coffee first," she said and looked at Joseph, raising her eyebrows.

He nodded.

Holly set about making coffee; her mother went on with her cookies, and Joseph leaned on the butcher block wondering whether these women were traumatized or not. In his opinion, they ought to be.

Heidi Banister was a good-looking woman in her forties. Her body moved with girlish lightness though her face remained still. She had a peculiar look around her mouth that Joseph interpreted as bitterness, maybe the trace of a marriage long gone rancid. She bent to put the cookies in the oven, then recalled it was not yet hot enough and straightened up. This made him aware of her body and, momentarily, he wondered whether she really could have slept with all the men her husband thought she did. Or any of them. She had faced a choice between the stasis of submission and the hazard of divorce, the life-threatening peril. Was she now retreating into a comfortably female kitchen-world? He felt he should try to talk to her, so he asked if she were also musical, like her two daughters.

"Just about tone-deaf," she said, sponging spots of batter off the counter. "And my husband's no better, though he claims he played bass in high school. With a band. They must have been terrible. No, it was my father who had the genes. You might have heard of him. Nathaniel Breitler?"

"Breitler! Of course I've heard of him. He was a first-rate pianist."

Heidi heaved a sigh and, though she appeared as impassive as ever, Joseph seemed to have broken through the ice jam. She leaned on the counter and spoke at length.

"First-rate is right, but, you know, he was never satisfied. His own toughest critic. It's hard to live with a perfectionist. You want to grab his collar and tell him to cut it out, tell him it's obsession, vanity, that it's-it's solipsism. He didn't demand perfection from us, from his kids-especially not from me, without any talent. In fact, he preferred me to my brother who was talented. Bruce loved the harpsichord. He's an investment banker now and maybe that's why-my father, I mean, setting such high standards for himself and none at all for his son. I once asked my mother how she could bear living with him. She patted my arm and said it wasn't difficult once you worked out that most of the time men are six-year-olds. What do you think?" She made a face at Joseph, not a mother's face but a judge's. "They never give up their toys-whether it's a piano or a gun."

Nonplused, Joseph said, "I have your father's recording of the late Beethoven sonatas."

The day was full of non-sequiturs. Nothing cohered.

"Coffee's ready." Holly turned from the counter to him. "Sugar? Cream? Milk?"

"A little milk."

"Two percent, one percent, buttermilk, skim, homogenized, pasteurized, almond, oat?" Why was she teasing him? Her mother had just declared all men to be infantile and possessive. She was off them herself.

"Do you think we could lend him some of Dad's clothes?"

"Oh, I don't know-"

"Really, it's not-"

"Why not? He can't wear-"

"It's just-"

"I'm fine, really-"

"No. You're not. And of course, you'll want a shower. I'll get you a towel."

"Oh, we have to put a plastic bag over that cast. Make it tight. You remember when Hadley broke-"

"Hadley. I nearly forgot. I really should-"

"Yes, you should. Go call her. I'll see to him."

"She's going to want to talk to you.   She's going to want to come home."

"You really think so?"

"Of course."

"Look, I don't want to be any-"

"I'll drive up and get her. It's not all that far."

"Well, if she really insists-"

"God. I would."

"Finally! The oven's hot."

It all sounded a little mad to Joseph, who still felt like an unwanted delivery left by the rhododendrons.

Holly took the phone into the living room. Meanwhile, Heidi fished out a garbage bag, gently took his arm out of its sling, pulled the bag over his cast, and made it tight with a tie. Then she herded him toward the stairway. He felt a bit like a failed pitcher, sent to the showers.

"I gather we're to keep an eye on you-though not, presumably, while you're showering. You'll be spending the night. No arguments. So there's still going to be a man in the house." She put a fresh towel and washcloth in his left hand and said she'd find him something to wear.

After showering, Joseph wrapped the damp towel around him as best he could and peered out the door. There he found a green Calvin Klein polo shirt, white socks, and a pair of blue jeans-too large in the waist-neatly folded on the floor.

Holly wasn't wrong about zippers.

4.

While Joseph was cleaning himself up, Holly phoned her sister who did indeed beg to be brought home. So, he would be having a late dinner with Heidi Banister "à deux," as she said.

"I spoke to Hadley, of course. Did all I could to soften matters. Reassured like mad. I told her to think of it as an episode, which always sounds so dismissible and self-contained-you know, as in 'you're just going through a stage.' Did your mother ever say that to you?"

"She did."

"I didn't mention the gun or even you. Holly'd done all that. . . and probably gave her an analysis of me, too. Do you know, there were times when I actually yearned for a little sibling rivalry. Those two are as thick as thieves."

Joseph thought it a peculiar wish but then Heidi Banister didn't seem inclined to exurban decorum. She was not a contented person. Maybe her husband's jealousy was exacerbated by her boredom and disappointment. He pictured the talented daughters with their heads together, fuller of Breitler genes than their father's.

Before dinner, Heidi sat on the living room couch, apparently at her ease, exactly as she had been not so many hours before when her husband was threatening to blow her away and she looked as if she didn't mind. She had made them both vodka tonics while the steaks she wanted him to grill defrosted.

She guessed the direction of his thoughts. "His name's Christopher. My husband. Christ-bearer. Saint Christopher was such a fraud even the Church eventually had to admit it. But, to be fair, Chris isn't a complete fraud, though I suppose you don't make as much as he does in real estate without a lot of fibbing. He inherited the business, though, so the really nasty work was done by his father, a real tough swamp Yankee. Amazing how quickly money gets clean nowadays. You don't even have to wait a whole generation. A little foundation will do the trick-and you save on taxes too."

Joseph sat in the very armchair into which he had collapsed after flooring Christopher Banister. There was a small blood stain on the carpet that he resisted covering with his foot.

"Holly told me who you are. Another musician. Odd that I should be surrounded by them, don't you think?" She sipped and sighed. "I like music but sometimes-"

"Yes?"

"Sometimes it feels like a wall, the kind that closes in." She waved her hand and laughed lightly at what she'd just said. "Oh, I don't know. It must be entirely different for you, more like it was for my father. You people move in a different world. You've got different gods too, don't you? Do you worship the greats?"

"I have my enthusiasms," he said guardedly.

She smiled at him, lifted her drink from the coffee table, girlishly drew her legs up under her, and adopted a tone at once amused and challenging. "If you tell me about your parents, I'll tell you about Holly's fiancé-the fiancé that was." Evidently, when it came to not missing things, Heidi Banister resembled Patrick Casillas.

"My father was a doctor, an internist. He died five years ago-heart attack, out of the blue. My mother worked for years in the medical field too, as what's called a hospitalist-"

"I know what a hospitalist is."

Joseph pressed on, as if testifying under subpoena. "After my father died, she retired and moved to California to be near my sister and her family. Julie's nine years older than I am and has two boys. Her husband's a partner in a Los Angeles law firm. I visit twice a year. Your turn."

If an armed and deranged husband who believed her promiscuously unfaithful was unable to shake her equipoise, Joseph's little challenge certainly wouldn't. The way Heidi Banister sipped her cocktail and lounged on the couch suggested nothing even remotely post-traumatic. To Joseph it appeared she was reserving judgment on him and might go on doing so forever. She clearly didn't feel obliged to pretend to like him. Why should she? He presumed she was sizing him up because of Holly. It made sense that she should. Her daughter had broken off her engagement and, within twenty-four hours, was rescued under dramatic circumstances by a man of a plausible age, tolerable appearance, and what Holly probably deemed an ideal, even a romantic profession. Even though she hadn't heard her daughter say she was off marriage rather than men, she was bound to think her daughter susceptible. Heidi would take a mother's view. Joseph was guilty until proven innocent-and what man is innocent?

She was in a mood to philosophize. "Perhaps," she began, "you've noticed how frequently people are wrong when they say relationships are built, as if they were pyramids or skyscrapers-or starlets. It's often the other way around. I mean the relationship's what's left over after a long process of unbuilding. You start with prejudices, misconstructions, suppositions, fantasies-with illusions that can seem as sturdy as an office block. Then there begins a kind of erosion or dismantling until you're left with what might, for lack of a better term, be called the truth. And usually more than one truth. There's the truth of the other person, the truth about yourself, and finally the truth about how things really are between you. Have you ever noticed that, Joseph? May I call you Joseph?"

"Certainly," he said, feeling like a small mammal suddenly realizing it was an experimental subject in a maze. It was an acidic analysis. "That's one view of how things develop between people. But you don't leave much room for them to be changed by each other, or by the relationship itself."

"Because people aren't, not really. Changed. That's just what I mean by illusion. When you're young and liberal, you're sure people can be changed; when you're my age, you don't. What strikes you then is how nothing seems to change them at all."

He couldn't help thinking of her husband. "Nothing?"

"Well, I won't rule it out absolutely. People can escape theories about people. But maybe you'll understand if I say that's how things went with Holly and Bradley, the unbuilding, I mean. You see, he's not a musician but he is a music-lover, a zealot. I think he fell for Holly because she is a musician, a fine one. Since he adores music and can't make it himself, he overestimates people who can, sees them as higher beings. Bradley's what's called a good man, solid through and through. He does something in finance. I wonder how anybody so scrupulous could manage in that world. But he seems to manage it just fine."

Joseph felt an urge to interrupt her. "He sounds like a paragon."

"Oh, yes. Williams College, Harvard B-School, plays rugby by the rules, dresses well. But paragons have their drawbacks," she said tartly. "They don't wear well. They can even wear away."

"Your daughter found him-dull? Is that what you mean?"

"Not so much dull but. . . predictable. It's not the same thing. Holly had just reached the point where her life seemed a question and Bradley looked like the answer. It happens to a lot of people-not just women-in their third decade. I don't doubt it was much the same for him. After all, isn't that why people marry? Suddenly they want to be grown-ups, to dress up, own bookcases, and play house. They want all those annoying adolescent emotional and sexual hang-ups settled once and for all. They get sick of the identity crisis and dating. Marriage is a great seducer, Joseph."

All this sagacity made him impatient and so he asked, "Was that how it was for you?"

She smiled at him, unperturbed by the question, and replied, "Naturally."

"So Holly and Bradley became-what?-disillusioned with each other?"

"Not with each other, no. I think Bradley's the type of man who could stay faithful to an illusion for a couple of decades at least. And Holly didn't change her view of him, or not exactly. I think what she came to see was that the only thing she could do with Brad was to disillusion him. These last months, well, what I saw was Holly working at doing just that and, in the end, what became unendurable for her was that she failed."

"So then Brad's still an answer, just the wrong one?"

"I think so. He's a very good answer but, to Holly, not the right one. She may yet regret it. Right answers aren't always good in the long run."

Heidi downed the last of her drink and got to her feet. "I think those steaks should be ready by now. What do you say to baked potatoes and a nice salad? Not feeling at all woozy, are you?"

Joseph also got up, a little awkwardly, because of his arm. "I'm fine," he said firmly.

Cooking took up their attention and lowered the tension. Over the meal, conversation was stop-and-go, ranging from his high opinion of Mahler to her favorite movies. It was the latter that led to the only thing Heidi said about the day's big event, or what led to it, and it shocked Joseph.

"You've seen Psycho, of course. The famous shower scene? You know, what always got me about it was how much Janet Leigh's character is enjoying that shower-I mean, she's entirely self-contained in her pleasure, out of the reach of detectives, bank managers, and lovers. It almost amounts to masturbation. Men just can't stand that sort of thing. They need to kill it."

"All men aren't like that," Joseph retorted though with less conviction than he'd have liked.

"Did I say all, Joseph? If so, I beg your pardon. That would be unpardonably rude."

Then the phone started to ring.

5.

They were doing dishes when the sisters pulled into the driveway a little past eight o'clock.

Hadley, a pretty, fresh-looking teenager with a rounder shape than her sister and luminous skin, ran in and threw herself on her mother with an exclamation that summed up her feelings.

"God, Mom!"

Then, without even looking at him, she hugged Joseph, being careful of his right arm. "Thank you, thank you, thank you," she whispered into his ear, as if her gratitude had to remain a secret between them.

Holly said nothing at all. She looked exhausted and dropped on to one of the stools by the counter.

Heidi asked what she could get them to eat.

"Eat? Who could eat? Anyway, we grabbed burgers on the road," Hadley reported with breathless contradiction. She grabbed her mother's hand. "Jeez! Have you seen the news? It was all over the radio. Have the TV people been here yet? The blondes with the microphones and idiotic questions?"

Holly explained to her sister why they hadn't yet been assaulted. "Remember that police car parked just outside the driveway?" Plutopia is protective of its property owners.

Hadley, dressed in jeans and a extra-large Harvard sweatshirt with sleeves that covered her hands, turned toward Joseph, who was at the sink. She pulled up her sleeve and pointed a finger at him. "And you!" she said with the excitement her mother and sister eschewed, "you're the hero." She struck a pose, one hip out, placed the finger she had aimed at Joseph on her plump cheek, and did a fair impression of a tough headline writer. "Hero-Composer Saves Distressed Damsels. Real Estate Tycoon Under Arrest and Under Observation. Exclusive Suburb in Shock. Neighbors say he was-"

Holly gently cut her off. "Enough, Had."

But the locomotive had too big a head of steam. "On the radio they even mentioned that I play the flute and Holly plays the violin," she said to Joseph. She took her mother's hand and said, "So, he finally went totally bonkers." Then she cried a little and dropped her mother's hand. Holly put her arm around her sister's shoulders.

"How's the concussion?" she asked. "Pass out or anything while I was away?"

"I'm okay, just fine. Really. You could've dropped me at home, though it was nice chatting with your mother and the food was delicious."

"And it was nice to have company," said Heidi, mimicking his tone.

The rest of the evening lasted barely an hour. As soon as Hadley's weepiness went away, she asked her mother a series of questions to which she received evasive answers. After that, the daughters were on their cell phones and Heidi went up to bed.

Between calls, Holly asked Joseph if he knew where he was to sleep. Then she coyly added, "My offer stands, by the way. About the orchestration. Thought about it?"

Joseph had thought about it and was sure he didn't require her help. So, when a grateful acceptance leapt from the tangle of his psyche he was as surprised as when he'd told Joyce he couldn't any longer do whatever this was.

"Good. We'll start tomorrow after I drive you home. Let's not forget your bike."

"What about your work?"

"What there is of it can wait."

The next day, however, what work got done was chiefly that of the ladies and gentlemen of the press.

6.

Christopher Banister was a bigshot and what had happened was news.

Two TV trucks were parked around the corner from Joseph's apartment building so that Holly, who was searching for a place to park, and Joseph, who was directing her while simultaneously explaining his perplexity about whether a certain obbligato passage should go to a violin or cello, missed seeing them.

They got out of the Lexus but there was no time to take his twisted bike out of the trunk before the reporters surrounded them. The scrum was less like sharks feeding than the raucous rush of descending pigeons. Everyone has seen the thrusting microphones, the sharp-elbowed reporters shouting out questions like accusations, the blank, bewildered faces of their targets. But when one of the reporters shouted to her cameraman that the blonde next to Joseph Tritto was Holly Banister the mob turned nearly mad. It was just too good. The questioning shifted from details of the rescue to the nature of their relationship. "It was just a coincidence," Joseph kept repeating this way and that, smiling all the while, but reporters care as little for coincidences as policemen. "Did you know each other, Joe? When did you meet?" "Were you going to the house to visit Holly?" "Did Christopher Banister say anything to you about his daughter before you decked him, Joe?" "Holly, is Joe here your knight in shining armor?"

Holly shrank in horror and Joseph did his utmost to keep his body between her and the poking microphones, the nosy cameras, the pushy questioners. He took Holly's right arm in his left hand and backed to the foot of the steps, following an atavistic instinct to keep the foe in front and make for high ground. He would have preferred to say nothing, to send them away with a curt "no comment," but knew this would be a mistake. Refusing to entertain questions from the press is like invoking the Fifth Amendment-it's your right but it means you're guilty.

He gave the briefest summary of the events of the previous day, explained that his broken arm was from the bike accident, explained why he had been an overnight guest at the Banister household, and that, with both bike and arm out of commission, Ms. Banister had graciously volunteered to drive him home.

"Give us a look at the bike, Joe?"

Once inside, Holly asked for some water and, while Joseph rushed to the kitchen to fetch it, she looked around.

"It's so. . ."

"So what?"

"So masculine." That was her verdict.

He handed her the water, left-handedly. "Is that good because its macho or bad because it lacks a woman's touch?"

"I honestly don't know," she said.

"Sorry about all that outside. I should have realized."

She sipped at the water. "Didn't occur to me either; I mean that we've become public property."

The bulb on Joseph's old answering machine was flickering angrily, another kind of noisy silence, one flash per message.

"Look at that," he said.

"Figures. I didn't get off the phone until almost midnight. Go ahead. Check your messages. I'll entertain myself."

"First I should call my mother."

"There's a good boy," said Holly, squatting down to examine a bookshelf.

Joseph's mother answered right away. "I'm just making breakfast," she said. "Three hours difference. Remember?"

She knew nothing about what had happened, so he had to tell her and reassure her he was fine. She asked if he needed her to fly east and, when he said no, made him promise to fax her a full medical report. "And call your sister, please."

Then he started in on the messages. Most were from reporters or the producers of local talk shows; even one of the networks had called.

"Wrong fifteen minutes," he cracked to Holly, who had left the books when she discovered the score of the Suite spread out on the table like an abandoned baby.

"What?"

"Warhol. Never mind."

Patrick had left three messages, each more urgent than the last. The first was the wryest.

"Jesus, Joseph. If what I'm hearing's true you went for a bike ride, walked smack into the middle of a domestic violence cliché, and came out the toast of the town. If you're free from heroics today, how about giving me a call?"

More calls came in while Joseph was on the phone. "Damned Call Waiting," he muttered.

Then Holly got a call on her cell. It was Hadley wanting to know when she'd be back and whether Joseph would be coming with her. She also said that Brad had called the house. When she told him Holly wasn't there, he asked her to put their mother on. "They talked for a long time," Holly reported her saying. Joseph noted that the paragon had not called Holly directly and thought it showed either admirable tact or a willingness to take the shrewd advice of his almost mother-in-law. He could hear Heidi counseling him, "Bide your time, Bradley."

Among the score of messages was none from Joyce, a fact about which Joseph felt half-a-dozen ways.

Finally, they were able to sit down with the score. Holly was examining it when yet another call came in.

Joseph looked at the Caller ID. "I have to take it. It's the fuzz."

"Mr. Tritto? Detective Harbaugh. We spoke yesterday."

"Yes, Detective?"

"I'll still need to talk to you again. I can come to you."

"Today? Right now?"

"No, no. It doesn't have to be today. In fact, I wanted to let you know that I've checked out your story."

"My story?"

"Well, your identity, the facts."

"You mean whether or not I knew the Banisters two days ago?"

Detective Harbaugh was silent, perhaps deciding whether to laugh. "Yes, that was more or less it," he said. "Also, we had to decide whether to charge you with breaking and entering. That's what Mr. Banister's lawyer rather vigorously suggested we do. Obviously, we declined."

"Then I'm in the clear?"

"So far as we're concerned."

"Thanks. Good to know."

Then Harbaugh struck a sour note. "Sure, you can go back to being a hero." It was an odd remark, grudgingly congratulatory.

Holly was watching Joseph closely.

"Detective, can you tell me how Mr. Banister is?"

The answer was evasive. "He's. . . he's in a facility. Awaiting arraignment."

 "Yes, but is he okay? Physically, I mean."

"You'll be hearing from us soon, Mr. Tritto. Just need to cross some T's and dot a couple of I's."

Holly frowned at him. Her eyes were dark blue. He sat down beside her and told her most of what the detective had said. She nodded. Joseph judged it best to leave out the breaking and entering business and the sour crack about his heroics.

A half-hour later he was still showing Holly the orchestration he had accomplished when there was heavy banging at the door and Patrick shouting through it, "My hair's blow-dried but I'm not from TV. Guess who." He was balancing two large pizzas, a couple of lemonades, and a six-pack of beer. He bustled in with this abundance wearing skin-tight designer jeans and his trademark red canvas high-tops and immediately reminded Holly that they had played together in a youth orchestra a decade earlier. "You were first violin and I was last, so of course I remember you." And that was the first time Joseph saw the serious Holly Banister smile. It was such a radiant experience that he didn't even mind not being its cause.

7.

They fell into a routine. Holly arrived for work at ten o'clock and left by four, as if it were a real job. In fact, Joseph had offered to make it just that, to pay her a fee; but she had looked at him in a way that made him regret the offer. He thought briefly of venturing a joke: "If it's not for money then it must be for love." But, as his head was now quite clear, he suppressed the impulse.

The third morning an exasperated Holly burst through the door complaining that her sister was jealous and bored and refusing to go back to the festival. "It's a serious matter. All her friends are away, and she's intensely interested in you."

Joseph went to get her a cup of coffee. "Why don't you bring her with you tomorrow? We can afford to take a break. We could go to a museum, take in a movie."

"She feels funny about leaving Mother on her own."

"And you don't," he said without thinking.

"Of course not. Hadley's just wallowing in adolescent guilt. It's because she wasn't there, and that weighs on her. It's silly. Mother loves being on her own. When we were kids and went off to summer camp, she practically did a jig. Besides, her girlfriends are beating at the door with curiosity and sympathy. She's a celebrity."

"And apparently a symbol, too."

Joseph was alluding to the shift in the relentless press coverage. Though the rescue story had run its course, displaced by a water main break, a five-car pile-up, and the arrest for fraud of one of the city's best-known philanthropists, the story lingered. It had been transformed into a topic for public debate. While Christopher Banister's lawyer had not succeeded in getting Joseph tossed in jail, he did get the charge against his client reduced to attempted assault, on the grounds that his client was the only person who was actually injured, that he had a license for the gun, that it was a first offense, that he was a pillar of the community. That provoked some controversy and the judge added more by letting Banister out on bail. But at the prosecutor's insistence, he did agree to a restraining order, forbidding the defendant from going anywhere near his wife.

Women's groups expressed their outrage. There were picketers in front of the courthouse, editorials in the newspapers, and lengthy interviews with academic experts on domestic violence and the psychology of batterers. Holly's only comment on this development was brief and rather cheerful: "At least the heat's off us."

The orchestration of the Suite proceeded smoothly and well. Joseph accepted all Holly's suggestions, especially about the strings, for which she even persuaded him to compose two new, challenging passages. He enjoyed the work itself as much as doing it with Holly. She grasped what he was after without needing any explanations. It would be difficult to say whether the work increased their attraction or if it was attraction that made the collaboration so agreeable. In any case, in a matter of days they had made more progress than Joseph had in a month, and this allowed them, so to speak, to pay more heed to the sexual tension between them.

When Hadley finally brought her sister with her, Joseph invited Patrick to join them for the day. The two took to one another the moment they met. Patrick offered a detailed, well-informed appreciation of Hadley's clothing, which looked uncoordinated and grungy, but was really high-end stuff. Patrick knew the names of all the designers and completely delighted Hadley by asking where she'd bought everything. They quickly established that they shared a love for the wind music of Darius Milhaud, the films of Pedro Almódovar, the Venetian mysteries of Donna Leon, and Euro-Techno. Hadley and Patrick had so much to say to each other that Joseph and Holly were left more to one another than if they had spent the day working instead of at the Institute of Contemporary Art, munching their way through the waterfront market, strolling in and out of upscale downtown galleries.

Hadley called her mother three times. "She's turned her phone off," she reported, sticking out her lower lip in a pretend pout. But she was in high spirits. Neither sister was concerned. "Tennis and gossip," Holly opined. "We'll try again later." Joseph wondered if it might be a boyfriend for whom the phone was switched off-if there really was one, even one.

After polishing off the galleries they returned to Joseph's apartment. It was getting near rush hour, but Hadley begged to stay. "Let's all have dinner together. I'm dying for a lobster. Come on. You wouldn't send me back into the wilds of ennui without a lobster, would you?" Holly phoned their mother to see if it was all right. There was still no answer, so she left a message.

They took the Lexus down to the waterfront where Hadley downed a two-pound boiled lobster. In a spirit of solidarity, Patrick did the same. Joseph had scallops and Holly baked scrod.

"Don't they look adorable in their bibs," Holly said to Joseph.

"Yes. Very cute. I feel almost parental. Elbows off the table, Patrick."

There was much laughter and the girls only spoke of their father once, when Hadley told Patrick he was camping out at a friend's beach house and wanted her and Holly to visit him the following weekend.

"Are you going to?"

Hadley giggled. "You kidding? Anyway, the festival winds up next weekend and I promised to be back on Monday for rehearsal. I'm first violin, you know."

"Ah," said Patrick lifting his beer, "like sister, like sister."

They dropped Patrick and Joseph off at eight-thirty and the sisters headed home.

Fifty-two minutes later Holly phoned Joseph.

Her voice was dry and flat. "She's dead. They both are. Hadley's hysterical. The police are on the way. Can you come?"

8.

They had made up their minds that the month of horror and mess would end, like summer itself, when the orchestra played the first notes of Joseph's Suite Populaire Américaine. None of them believed that matters would really improve just because a date had been reached, because of mere music; but they kept saying it would for one another's sake.

Holly had become motherly toward her sister who, for two weeks, had endured fits of crying, black withdrawal, but also two days of manic euphoria.

Now Hadley was seated up in the mezzanine between her best friend Julie Murphy and Patrick Casillas. Holly sat beside Joseph, three rows from the stage. The polite noises of the crowd, the buzz of life, felt comforting. Joseph's cast had been gone for a week but when-in the silence out of which music issues-he took Holly's left hand in his right one she pressed her lips against his ear and whispered, "Don't squeeze. It's too soon."

www.ingramcontent.com/pod-product-compliance
Lightning Source LLC
Chambersburg PA
CBHW022130150726
47992CB00002B/527